SO-AKS-388

ILLUS. COLL.

for reference:

not to be
taken from CHILDREN'S
this area

vancouver
public
library

7B

CARNEGIE MEDAL

1961 Boston, L.M.

A stranger at Green Knowe

A Stranger at Green Knowe

by the same author

*

THE CHILDREN OF GREEN KNOWE
THE CHIMNEYS OF GREEN KNOWE
THE RIVER AT GREEN KNOWE

..... *such strange things as the Moon* ...

A Stranger at Green Knowe

L. M. BOSTON

illustrated by
PETER BOSTON

FABER AND FABER
24 Russell Square
London

First published in mcmlxi
by Faber and Faber Limited
24 Russell Square London WC1
Printed in Great Britain by
Latimer Trend & Co Ltd Plymouth
All rights reserved

J
cop. 2

© by Lucy Maria Boston
1961

ILLUS. COLL.

Contents

Part One

Imagine a tropical forest so vast that you could roam in it all your life without ever finding out there was anything else. Imagine it so dense that even if a man flew over it for hours, his aeroplane bumping on the rolling uplifts of heat, he would see nothing but the tops of trees from horizon to horizon. It is in such a forest that this story must begin. It is a far flight, both in distance and in imagination, from the dewy meadows and long history of Green Knowe to this primeval and almost immortal forest in the Congo. The journey however can be made, but not in a hurry.

To look for the hero of the story you must venture into the haunted gloom of the forest. Even at noon it is dark like a heavily curtained room, and at night like a closed oven. From among the roots of the trees ropes of creeper loop up, weighing the leaf ceiling down and tying trees together, sometimes knitting square miles into an unbroken tangle. Elsewhere at the rocky foot of a cliff a dell might be damp and mossy with giant ferns. If the sun finds a chink where it can slip a live ray down through the arcaded branches, it lies on the moss like an emerald. A moonbeam glitters like a bone, a tooth, or the white of an eye. A terrible silence warns explorers to keep out.

What lives there? Nobody really knows. Some say gods, some say devils, some say the souls of their ancestors, but certainly it is the home of mysterious creatures nearer to man than anything yet discovered—the awe-inspiring gorillas. On the fringe of the forest or by the bed of a stream an adventurous native hunter might sometimes find the print of a foot fifteen inches long. Such near meetings between cousins would be unwelcome to both. A native gorilla hunt into the inner forest rarely took place. When it did so, it was an affair involving whole tribes, and was so full of terror and the cruelty bred by terror, that it needed all the native magic of drums, dances, offerings, prayers and charms to see it through. They felt it as an assault on one of the forest gods to steal his power for themselves. Among the hunters would be warriors covered with glory, trackers of genius and chieftains' sons, but none of these is the hero of this book. The forest has deeper recesses where the silence is as old as time itself.

Though this is the hottest place in the world, it is not, as one might think, scorched and dry. On the contrary it is steaming and dripping like an overheated greenhouse built on a compost heap. It smells spicy and pungent, of growing and rotting. The atmosphere round the Equator, bullied by the relentless sun close overhead, works up almost daily through suffocating heat into thunderstorms worthy of the beginning of the world, and torrential rain more penetrating than the sun, against which even the forest gives little shelter. The many rivers and rivulets that run in ravines through the forest dry off to little more than steaming mud, then fill up overnight and empty themselves in spate. The waterfalls whisper one day and roar the next, tumbling over a cliff among low clouds, but so thickly matted is the jungle that it is not until one breaks out of it at the water's edge that the sudden sound is heard.

Whoever lives here must surely have qualities to catch the imagination and a grandeur to inspire love. It is the very place for a hero and here he is, though still very young—a two year

...the print of a foot fifteen inches long......

old gorilla living in the immense privacy of the forest with his family. It consisted of his father, his father's three wives, and seven children not counting the new baby. Gorillas develop more quickly than humans, so this small furry person was like a child of five. Like a boy of that age he could and did plague his mother, though not the baby, but his father was the object of his veneration. The Old Man was a splendid creature, almost twice the size of his wives, powerful beyond belief, and amiable enough if not crossed. He was dictatorial. The elder boys got cuffs from him that really taught them to respect him, but he would play with the little ones and sometimes sit them on his knee or carry them on his shoulders.

They lived on the ground, using the branches of trees to swing themselves over obstacles, but usually travelling along tunnels in the undergrowth, the Old Man going first to tear and trample a way. He knew the country and its rivers and animal paths. He knew where to look for food at different seasons—roots, pithy canes, succulent stems, fruit and nuts. To the young gorilla the earth was as familiar and dependable as his mother. It was alive, it was bountiful, its fur of mosses and leaves was always brushing against him, sheltering him from sun and rain. It was warm and soft under his feet, it had a pervading reassuring exciting smell. It was always the same and yet full of surprises. He ate, as a matter of course, the canes he lived among, like Hansel and Gretel eating their toffee-and-barley-sugar house. His toys were fern leaves or feathers which he put on his head, imitating his father who often covered his head when he snoozed; or sticks to bang with, or swings of tough creeper stems; or he pelted his brothers with anything that came to hand, or played with them the really important game of Disappear, at which his giant father was an expert, vanishing without a sound. This was an art that every gorilla must learn young. It was their best defence. Instinctively perhaps a baby guessed that to be alive is to be in danger, though it was difficult to imagine any in their private paradise. But the Old Man knew, and his authority impressed them.

Gorillas, unlike the four-handed monkeys, have real feet, though with thumbs, and can easily either walk and stand upright or gallop on all fours, in which case they use the knuckles of their hands like hoofs. Very often they sidle, using one arm as a foreleg and keeping the other free for any use proper to hands. This gives them a movement rather like side-stroke, smooth and effective for passing through their shadowy forest element where there may be no room for a gallop. Disappear and Catch were endless games.

Other creatures lived in the forest too, birds and butterflies and monkeys. At the top of the trees there was a commotion at sunrise and sunset, but that didn't affect the little gorilla. It was a likeable noise a long way off up there, and the birds when they came down to drink at the streams were brightly coloured things that blended with the perpetually flickering chinks of sunlight. Occasionally near a stream a herd of elephants would pass the gorilla family, would recognize them with a wink from their jolly little eyes and a twitch of their sail-like ears but otherwise take no notice. There was plenty of room and green food for everyone. The elephants trampled down wide spaces where the fun of chasing one's brothers, vaulting over fallen trees, was sharpened by a rather creepy excitement because it was naked to be away from the encircling contact of high ferns and leaves. In the clearing left by the elephants he saw such strange things as the moon, both in the sky and in the water; discovered how wet rain was without even a leaking forest umbrella and also how crushingly hot the sun.

The gorilla family was always on the move, eating the best as they went. The forest closed up after them and everything grew as before. It was a leisurely life. Though the young ones, as children will, ate all the time, the family scattered in the morning to collect armfuls of food, the Old Man grunting so that no one should stray too far until they re-gathered to sit round and eat what they had brought. There was very little squabbling. Enjoyment was the order of the day, and food was eaten with good manners and an exchange of appreciative comments. The skins and stalks and left-overs were laid in a tidy pile beside each eater. At midday the Old Man had a snooze. That was because he was on guard at night.

They moved on a few miles, every day, but sometimes the Old Man, peering and listening, decided to make a quick march. Then they might travel all day thrusting ever deeper into the hot green shadow, the Old Man with his prodigious arms and shoulders tearing the ropelike stalks or breaking off boughs.

As a family they were rather silent, but the wives did sometimes chatter. Gorillas have muzzles, in that more resembling horses than men, and the conversation of the young ones is a soft whinnying when excited. Secrets however are exchanged with heads close together and no noticeable movement of lips or nostrils. The Old Man's word was law, and instantly understood by all. Generally it was grunts or snuffles or sniffs—with which a very great deal can be said; all that is needed for family life. Sometimes he uttered near-words in a clear baritone, but that was only when he was standing upright. On all fours grunts are easier. Then there was his terrible growl, not to be lightly provoked, though he did it sometimes to the little ones as a game to make them scatter, and they in turn practised it as best they could on each other.

The young males spent a lot of time having mock battles, defying and chasing each other in turn, or scuffling over and over with their mouths wide open in a kind of laughing ferocity. Our little gorilla had a half-sister near his own age to whom he was attached. His secrets were for her. They generally ate side by side, sharing what they found, though perhaps she gave it to him oftener than he to her.

Every night the gorilla family camped in a new place. There is no lingering twilight at the Equator. The camp must be chosen before sunset, or darkness would suddenly overtake them. Often the sun would be covered in close haze all day, but as it always sets at the same time the animals know the rhythm of equal day and night. In the thickest forest here and there was a tree so huge and roofy as to keep an open territory for itself. The Old Man would choose some such sheltered clearing, examine it for snakes, and the making of his bed would be the sign for the others. They broke down branches to make a springy foundation and then heaped leaves on top rounding them into a loose nest. The Old Man, who was very heavy, paid great attention to his bed, holding a strong sapling down with his foot while he reached for another to twist under and round it so that the springs of his bed inter-locked. This he did in a circle to make a framework. The others each made his or her own, the young ones often in the trees. Less skill is needed with a good forked branch as a foundation. The little ones did their best to make something like a bed but if it was lopsided they got in with mother and the baby after all. Perhaps they would no sooner be in, than the gloomy green of the forest would grow rapidly darker, the glimmer die right away and total velvet darkness blot out everything and seem to touch the eyes. Then the Old Man's grunts were most reassuring. On clear nights, when the chinks between the top leaves, that had shown blue, suddenly showed stars, the forest would be darker than by day certainly, but would still be dimly there, trunks and masses of leafage just discernible but not so that one could be sure nothing was there that should not be. Or perhaps the moon would spread out patches of white that lurking "things" would be careful not to cross, so that the one place that could be seen focussed all the fear of the dark. All the family was asleep, like the birds, the little forest deer, the forest pigs, and the millions of flies, all hushed.

Very occasionally in the night there might be a leopard's yellow eyes looking down from a branch above, straight into the bright nervous eyes of a little gorilla, but the Old Man was nearby, turning in his bed. He did not even trouble to growl. The leopard simply knew and took no risks. There are plenty of young things to kill who haven't got such a formidable guardian. It was not so much the Old Man's bite that was to be feared, though that was deadly, but his slashing, tearing arms, his bull's weight. With his width of chest he could tear a leopard apart. He could also, for a short distance, springing, swinging and bouncing as no other creature of like weight, move as fast as a leopard burdened with its prey. After the leopard had plopped softly to the ground and gone off, the mother gorillas rocked the squeaky long-armed infants at their breasts with murmurous loving grunts, not entirely without anxiety. In the morning sometimes for a dare a youngster got into the Old Man's bed after he had left it. It had a musky clinging Old Man smell. If you wore that smell in your fur, you were Somebody.

In the Old Man's bed you were Somebody

The Old Man, superb and invincible as he seemed, had nevertheless two kinds of enemy. Our little gorilla was to see them both. The nearest was his own eldest brother. As in all the royal families of ancient history, the heir is likely to be ambitious and troublesome, and the second son jealous of the first and willing to make trouble between him and his father. For all full-grown gorillas are natural kings. As with humans, the usual thing is for the grown sons to choose a wife and go away with her to found another tribe, and in fact no traveller or hunter has ever heard, or seen, or found traces of a serious fight between two gorillas. Family squeals and scuffles of course are frequent enough. But boys will be boys, and bad boys crop up everywhere. Our little gorilla's eldest brother was presumptuous and proud. A grunt was no longer enough for him to obey; it had to be followed up by a frown and a snarl from his father. This was more than enough for the treacherous leopard, but the more the son was threatened the more resentful he became. He was nearly as big as his father though not so heavy, and he knew his own self-will but did not know what reserve force lay beneath the Old Man's rather lazy dignity. Every day there was some little incident that caused his mother to sniff and click and the other wives to squeal and mutter to each other. The little gorilla and his sister were shocked and frightened. To them the Old Man was a very great person. They were right to think so. A little gorilla has bright eyes and a gentle lively funny face. He has a comical shock of hair above his naked face, and the rest of his body is covered with long thin puppy hair. A full-grown male may be six feet in height and weigh thirty stone or more. His face is coal black and majestic with a high crest like a Roman helmet. His eyes are deep set and far seeing, but neither sly nor cruel. He is superbly dressed in dense fur, different for the three parts of his body. Over his shoulders and arms he wears a kind of matador's jacket of long glossy black bearskin, open at the throat to show his bare chest. He has a cummerbund of silver grey, and his legs are covered in beautiful thick opposum. He has all the dignity and decency that chimpanzees so outrageously lack. To a little gorilla he was the one splendid figure in the world, the leader, the protector, the avenger, and of course as all fathers sometimes are in private, the big dangerous joke.

One stiflingly hot morning, the worst after a week of crushing heat, electrically prickly with the streams drying up and no breath of air in the forest, which even in daylight is dark and stuffy like a tent, the family left their nests, shook the broken twigs and leaves out of their fur and stretched and scratched themselves in the trampled compound of their camp. The small ones swung down from the trees and dropped into the musky smell of bodies which was the family bond. When they were all assembled the Old Man led them off to find water. They were thirsty, for the previous day had been unlucky, the water too muddy to be refreshing. They travelled more quickly than usual in a strung-out procession. The Old Man was at the head, the mothers and children next and the half-grown males bringing up the rear. The eldest son's position by right was that of rearguard captain on peaceful excursions, to see that no stragglers were left behind. Had it been a retreat, his position and his father's would have been reversed. On this occasion he left his post, passing, with a boastful swing of his shoulders, his brothers, none of whom was old enough to have developed the adult crest. He jostled his way through the mothers and youngsters till he was behind his father in the forefront. A growling order to go back where he came from was disobeyed, but by now they could all smell the water and were making watery noises of anticipation to each other, though they could not as yet see the stream through the tangle. The Old Man tore down matted ropes of creeper to let them through, and when the little gorilla came there he saw the bed of a river sloping down in smooth dry stones to a sparkle of living water in the middle. It was fed by a white streak falling over a cliff and the banks were closed in by high trees covered by a twining curtain of hanging flowers. It made an amphitheatre with a cobbled floor, broken here and there by flat boulders, silent except for the echoing splash of the fall. Across this basin the Old Man was moving, followed closely by his unruly son, who, as his father crouched to drink, deliberately jostled him and drank first. He received for his insolence a slashing blow that toppled him over, while the Old Man towered to his full standing height, his threatening arms raised, and let out the gorilla battle roar which all hunters agree is the most terrible sound in the wild world, worse than the lion's roar. The little gorilla heard it now for the first time and his blood ran cold with panic and admiration. Grown-ups could do that! The gorilla tribe in consternation drew aside in a ring to watch, the females shaking their heads and making nervous sounds, the other young males tensed as if at the ready for a race. The battle at first was alternate charges, where the charger swerved at the last minute to deliver a scything stroke with his hooked nails. If the opponent stood his ground he might get off with nothing worse than a gash. But as the combatants grew angrier, and the Old Man's face was hideous with fury, the younger lost his judgement for an instant, and instead of side-stepping he turned tail in an effort to put another yard or two between them. Instantly the Old Man was on his back, teeth sunk in his shoulder muscles, and the arms that were strong enough for tearing up trees were now used to wrap him round. The two of them rolled over and over among the smooth stones of the river bed which made a rattling kettledrum sound as they slid under the struggling feet. The young males squealed and dashed round the edge biting and cuffing one another at random in their excitement. When at last the awe-inspiring wrestling match broke apart, the usurper had had enough. He bolted, trailing a wounded arm, to the other side of the river and disappeared into the trees. The Old Man then coolly finished his interrupted drink, and the rest of the tribe came humbly and dutifully to take their turn. The wives who had been silent during the fight now had much to say and some squealing and backbiting went on among them, something like "It was your son"— "It was the fault of your daughter"—"Don't you say anything against my family". It does not need words with grammar to convey such remarks. Meanwhile the Old Man sat splashing water over himself and looking very much in control of affairs. Finally they went back into the forest with keener appetites to get their breakfast, all but the defeated rebel. And when it came to resting time that night, one of the younger females was absent. She had found a chance to slip off and join him.

All this made a great impression on our little gorilla, who shared a nest with his favourite sister. It is a great future to be an Old Man gorilla. He put an arm round his little sister's neck and they held feet while the overdue storm pounded refreshingly on the distant tree-roof and ran down the trunks. Lightning played over the unseen sky, a mere shudder of light penetrating the trees. Thunder rolled a fanfare in praise of strength. The air was strong, embracing and odorous, the close drumming and dashing of the rain like an extra curtain of safety drawn round them. He could hear his father grunting as he shifted his bed under a hollow tree where the rain would not run down his neck. His wounds were stiffening after the fight and he wanted to get comfortable. He might have been saying "Silly young cub! What did he take me for?" And so the family went to sleep, heaped with leaves to keep them dry. No little boy tucked up in bed could feel more secure than a little gorilla tucked in by a seemingly endless forest, dreaming of happy games on its soft rich floor, where every day's direction is fresh and untrodden, all their own. How should he guess there was in fact a boundary to his world, outside which was a very different one, inhabited by vicious greedy second cousins who know no mercy toward the other side of the family?

The rain having come went on for weeks. The mossy ground squirted underfoot, dry gullies became streams, streams became rivers, rivers grew to tumultuous stampeding seas. Every green thing grew and swelled visibly and filled with sap. It was a time of luscious food.

In this rich season, the Old Man led them to higher country. They travelled a leisurely few miles every day. Why should they hurry? Wherever they happened to be they found plenty to eat. When the forest grew sparser from time to time they came on open rock-strewn ridges between richly wooded valleys. Distant mountains loomed as if floating in the sky. The Old Man, sitting in the shadow of a rock on such a hillocky ridge, looked round with pleasure at a landscape he recognized and had purposely come back to. If a gorilla has on the whole less consciousness than a man, nevertheless it is possible to be deeply happy without knowing it, as every human being discovers in time. And perhaps a gorilla too, since their memories are excellent. These excursions into open land and long views must be as refreshing to dwellers in the stuffy overcrowded forest as a day at the sea to human or canine town dwellers. They were thrilling travels for youngsters, electrified with fresh smells, new tastes, sharp hill breezes, sparkling colours. There were adventures such as the ascent of low cliffs, helped by the ropes of lianas, or rock scrub, or treacherous ill-rooted trees. Over really difficult ground the Old Man would take a youngster on his back. The wives of course always carried the latest baby, but they watched and helped the next youngest.

Rocks and boulders were fun. Rocks, sharp overhanging and ledgy, had the spice of fear. A ledge was a place from which the disappearing trick was difficult. A little gorilla who found himself on one would come down again quickly, rich with the experience of adventure. Hide-and-seek round boulders was a faster game than among trees and tangle, and had to be played on all fours without help from swinging ropes. He soon got out of breath. Boulders are warm and smooth, with cracks across their contours, and a friendly skin-like surface that feels alive. The little gorilla caught lizards by the tail. They wriggled wildly for his amusement, and on being released did their disappearing trick into a crevice. When he crouched to bring his eye to the crack, deep down inside he could see the lizard's eye flat and round like some sort of polished seed, hardly recognizable as an eye till it blinked.

One morning the little gorilla was eating breakfast beside his mother when he noticed that she had stopped eating to watch something attentively. He looked in the same direction and saw that the Old Man had stopped eating too and was turning his head this way and that and grunting as if displeased. He got up, leaving his food except for a bit of cane that was sticking out of his mouth as he chewed, and slipped through the undergrowth out of sight. Silence fell on the assembled family except for a grunt or two of curiosity. After a while the Old Man came back. Everyone could see that his normal indolence was gone, some order was to be expected from him. However he grunted that they were to go on with their meal. It was eaten more quickly than usual, not because he told them in so many gorilla grunts to hurry up, but because they all watched him and could see for themselves signs of impatience. Usually he made sounds of enjoyment as he ate. He even guzzled. But now he was only eating because it was the time for it, and his great head was still listening. When the meal was over, except for the slowest or greediest, he marshalled his family with an impatient cuff here and there, placed the two eldest of his remaining sons in the rear, and set off in the opposite direction from the one they had been taking, striking downhill again towards the thicker cover of the valleys. The little gorilla was sorry to be dragged away from the open country that had promised such an interesting variety of games and experiences, but if he lagged behind, his mother would call him, or one of his rearguard brothers jostle him on.

That day they travelled twice as far as usual, with only a pause for the Old Man's midday snooze. At sunset they chose their camp half-way down the side of the valley. One of the young wives who was lightly built and nervous made her nest higher up than usual in a tree above the Old Man's bed. Gorillas like to lie in bed late, especially if the day is cloudy or misty. They are comfortable animals and enjoy life. The following morning was just the weather for turning over and going to sleep again. The forest was swathed in mist which thickened to cloud at the tree tops. It was dark like a room with drawn curtains, and the faint sun when it came seemed only to make the mist more opaque. Nevertheless the young wife after much cracking of twigs in her nest, slid down her tree with a nicker of uncertainty that woke the Old Man. He rolled out of bed, bouncing on to all fours at the ready. Then he stood upright with his hand on the tree collecting his thoughts and taking stock of the situation before going quietly off to make his tour of inspection.

On his return he was authoritative and brusque, and they were moving on almost before the little ones could scramble out of their nests. This time the older sons led the way along the side of the valley and the Old Man brought up the rear, moving to left and right in ceaseless vigilance, though little could be seen and the fog blanketed hearing as well as sight. After they had gone a good distance, he sent the little wife up again to reconnoitre from the top where sound travels more freely. When she came down satisfied that there was nothing, they stopped to eat, which the little ones did ravenously, and even the Old Man, relieved in his mind, reassured them all with his usual grunts of satisfaction. All the same, they continued their trek through the mysterious shrouded trees, the elders grunting so that the little ones should not lose them. And woe to any small straggler who got under the Old Man's feet. He would be taught where he should be.

They covered that day ten miles of difficult country, double the distance of the day before, and not only ten miles of distance were between them and whatever they were avoiding, but a ten-mile density of cloud. As the light failed and the mist turned from pallid green to indigo-grey without lifting, discipline was relaxed. Beds were made with something like chatter among the females and bedtime fun for the little ones, for though they were tired the mere fact of bedtime reminded them that they had still some energy not used up. There was enough for some teasing and practical joking about each others' beds, and general chasing round.

The next morning was a lovely day, but even the young ones could tell that something was in the air. To start with, in the early dawn birds in the valley below had flown out of their roosting places passing on cries of alarm to each other. There was a stream down there, where the gorilla family would be going to quench their morning thirst. The birds should be drinking, lifting their bills to let the water trickle down, taking time to fluff out their feathers after a dip and to enjoy the private morning. In the slumbrous silence of the forest a bird crashing through the leaves was a rattle of alarm. The gorilla women squealed soft interrogations. The Old Man on all fours stood like a wide awake rock if such a thing can be imagined, his head and shoulders jacked up by his long arms, his elbows turned slightly out bringing into play the immense shoulder muscles. His deep-set eyes were bright with calculation. He made rapid turns to each point of the compass to listen, and at a toss of his head, the tribe was hushed. Then from the direction of the stream a leopard bounded through the camp. Its narrow body passed through the undergrowth like an eel through water-weeds. There was no sound except the heavy velvet landing of its forefeet after a leap. It went straight on uphill, not acknowledging the gorillas by so much as a glance. It was making off. The Old Man made sure that his party was assembled and ready, then he himself slipped off in the direction from which the leopard had come.

Suddenly from the bottom of the valley rose up a repeated sound that our little gorilla had never heard before, and to which he could give no meaning, except that it was thuds and strange vibrations. Something was striking something. This was followed by a crash that he recognized as a tree falling. His father often pulled down young trees, and elephants pushed over much larger ones. The Old Man came back in the worst possible temper. He cuffed them into marching order and started them off uphill parallel with the stream, avoiding the track they had made the day before. It is difficult in the densest forest to hear anything at a distance, or, even if it is not far away, to tell just where it comes from. Without breaking cover a general idea of what is going on is impossible. The stream that ran down the valley was in low water and its dry bed made an open causeway through their territory. They could not leave it altogether, because later on, higher up its course, they must drink. Sound travels upward, so that the rhythmic blows followed by crashes could still be heard far down stream, but growing fainter, and now almost inaudible. They had gone fast and were slackening the forced speed when the leopard crossed their path again, turning back from the direction he had tried. His ears were flattened, his flanks drawn in. He chose the direction they were taking and slipped on ahead, every inch of him jittery and suspicious. By now it was clear that something was seriously wrong. The Old Man was very active, circling rapidly and soundlessly round his flock, generally in the rear, but now and again coming forward to check up on the direction to be taken. The young leaders tended to drop towards the stream because they were thirsty. The Old Man was the first to realize that the faint tree-felling sounds were now coming, not from behind borne on the wind, but from ahead, faint because the wind was carrying the sound away. They were in fact far too near.

The Old Man was now fighting angry, but also worried.

He had tried three directions and found them too dangerous for his family. His crest was up, his brows frowning, his nostrils dilated and quivering. His stance was taut and commanding. It was right about turn, but not in the track they had already made where they had taken the easiest way for speed. Now they went in single file into the densest thickets, each gorilla slipping through the hole made by the young leader, while the Old Man brought up the rear again, not in the tunnel made by the others, but just to one side of it where he could see any pursuers without being seen. The order of the moment was concealment—the ultimate reason for the game of Disappear so often practised. Still hungry, still thirsty, they came to a clump of tough sturdy trees whose lower branches were so smothered in a weight of tangled creeper that anyone in the trees must be entirely hidden from an enemy below. Here they went into hiding. Even the Old Man found branches that would take his weight without cracking. High up in one of these same trees was the leopard again, flattened along a branch to look like the thickness of it, his usually twitching tail as still as wood. He was close above the little gorilla and his sister, but so clearly concerned about his own skin, not anybody else's, that they took no notice of him.

The tree felling had at last stopped, but other more alarming sounds had taken its place, hair-raising sounds from an unknown, unimaginable source, yells worse than any animal could make, clangs and rattles and thuds that were not in nature. The little gorilla hugging his sister felt the creeping almost ecstatic excitement of fear. It was new to him. He saw the adults' heads turning this way and that, their eyes searching beyond the leaves. He heard his mother's teeth chattering, and when her baby, infected by the general uneasiness, began to howl, she pressed its face into her shoulder to smother the sound. Our little gorilla watched his father and tried to imitate him, tried to dilate his nostrils, to pull the same fierce face. His father was wise and obviously knew what he was going to do next. What a great chest he had! He scratched it, and the little gorilla scratched his own and felt braver.

The blood-chilling noise came nearer, drawing in from three sides. Shrill throaty sounds, not explosive like the roar of a lion, not passionate like the trumpeting of a bull elephant, nor harsh like flesh-eating birds, but weak and reedy; and yet terrifying because of the repeated rhythm that caught at the heart, and because of a hateful quality of malice and triumph not known among the animals. The bushes were agitated with crashing sticks. Maybe this herd, whatever it was, would pass underneath them. But suddenly something pinged into the bole of the tree just by the little sister's foot—a slender stick with feathers quivering at the end. Then another. Then a heavy stick with a hard shining tip flew up, tilted over, and fell rattling down among the branches. The Old Man, angered and insulted beyond bearing, decided that now was the time for action to rout these troublesome insolents. He leapt to the ground and burst through the thicket with his thunder and his battle roar, a single tremendous champion against a hunting pack. The little gorilla was jigging on his branch with excitement, but there came a bang as shattering as a crack on the head, and then so terrible an increase in the yells, the dancing, the drums, the pans banged on kettles and such a surge of shiny-bodied black creatures that the gorillas fled helter-skelter in panic in the only direction open to them—downhill towards the river. Only the leopard remained motionless in his tree, unnoticed by the wild mob that danced and shrieked past him. When the lost and leaderless gorillas had gone a little way, they came to the clearing that had been made by felling the trees, and beyond it a stockade of trunks. The beaters pressed behind them, forcing them all to break cover and run for it. Some of the younger wives and half grown sons got over the stockade. The little gorilla and his sister pelted after their mother, but there was another bang and she stumbled and fell and lay still. The baby was still in her arms, but it had an arrow through it. While they wavered, stunned by the noise and with no one to lead them, two of their attackers rushed in with a rope net and threw it over them. The little gorilla tried to throw it off or bite his way through, but his enemies leapt upon him, and the squirming netful was tackled and overpowered at last three to one. He and his sister were trussed up and shoved breathless and palpitating into a cage. Some of his captors were black, but their Old Man as he seemed, had a red hairy face and red hairy arms. It was he who cut the cords of the net so that in their cage they could move if they wished. But they huddled together in a corner and hid their faces, frightened into a stupor. Crowds came to look at them, jabbering, laughing and poking, but always moving away towards a caterwauling that grew louder minute by minute beyond the abandoned clump of trees; from whence came now a straining scrum dragging a great weight. The little gorilla, catching a whiff of the familiar and reassuring smell had a fleeting dream of rescue and raised his face from his sister's neck to look. He saw the body of his chief and father laid out in the clearing, pulled and pushed in pitiful passivity. The red-faced man stood beside it with his bang stick while a war dance formed, circled and stamped and yelled, round and round it. He hid his face again, shivering. He wound his arms tighter round his companion but she hardly moved.

32

They huddled together in a corner and hid their faces.

C

Later a pole was pushed through the top of the cage from end to end, and swinging from that they were carried off in procession, first along the bed of the stream and afterwards along one of their own old tracks where whimpering they recognized their sleeping places. Where had all the family gone? The last sight of the Old Man inert and propped up by his puny enemies, was printed for ever on his memory. It made no sense but shock and despair.

Sadness and hunger and thirst filled his mind, and after a while, as he was jogged endlessly along in his cage, hunger and thirst only. He had had nothing all day and was an infinitely wretched ball of fur. Towards evening the cage was set down on the outskirts of a clearing where his captors had their camp. They scattered chattering and joyful to fetch water, make a fire, and prepare food. For a while there was no one near him, and the bush was but a little way off. He tried the bars, shook the framework and strained at the door with all the strength he had left. He bit at the cold hard stuff in despair. In his reckless efforts he overturned the cage, and made such a rattling that it brought the red-faced hairy man to look at him. He had a companion of the same kind. They answered his squeaky baby growls with unaggressive noises, and pushed some bananas through the bars. He was too thirsty now to take any interest in food. He went and sat by his sister, who had taken no part in his struggle to escape.

"Fine little chap," said his captor. "I suppose it's a male by the fight he put up. It's quite unbelievable how strong they are even at that age. I threw myself on top of the net, but it was all I could do to hold him. It took three of us to get them into the cage. I suppose they're thirsty. I know I was! Try some milk."

34

They slipped a dish between the bars and filled it from a bottle. As the liquid blop-blopped out of the neck the gorilla opened and shut his mouth. He was too dry to dribble or swallow, but he made no move towards the milk until the men came round to poke his sister in the back. Then he edged away from them and accidentally put his hand in the dish. He sucked his fingers, and couldn't help himself—he dabbled them back for more.

"He'll do," said the second man, "but you'll never rear the other, Blair. I've seen them like that before. They just turn their faces to the wall and die. Nothing you can do with them. Get the cage pegged so that he can't overturn it and leave them alone to settle down. Give them some leaves to make a bed."

"What shall we call the infant Hercules? There are too many Congos, but to call them George or Albert seems an insult to their fathers. Hercules is too long."

"Why not Hanno—the Carthaginian Johnny who saw one in the sixth century B.C.?"

"O.K. That's him. Dido for the other?"

"You needn't bother to christen her. She won't need a name."

When they had gone, Hanno as he must now be called, had most of the milk, and then put his milky fingers against his sister's lips. She licked them but did not open her eyes. He felt better after the drink, and as no one was looking, he eventually took the bananas, scuttling back to his sister and sitting with his arm round her shoulder making the loudest possible eating noises by her ear. When he had eaten the first with great relish he offered her the skin. She would not have it, so he ate it himself. After he had eaten several more he peeled one and

35

offered her the fruit. This was generous. She made a little dismal sound and huddled tighter into her corner. Hanno finished all the bananas and felt better. Presently the second man came back with leaves and straw which he stuffed through the bars.

"There you are, Hanno, you black-faced imp. Make yourself a bed of that."

Hanno did not move till he had gone. Then he seized an armful of leaves and heaped them over his sister and himself, so that at last they were hidden from strange eyes, however insecurely, and like an exhausted child he fell asleep.

The next day the travelling cage was carried into the shade of a tree and the door left open. As soon as the men were at a distance, Hanno gave his sister a tug and shot out to reconnoitre. Between him and the nearest bushes he ran against a hard mesh that he could not tear or bite. He tried to climb over, but there was a roof of it too. Nowhere could he find a hole. While he was hanging on under the roof, his two captors came in with food and drink which they put down. Hanno dropped down to hide behind the cage where his sister lay unmoving in the straw. The men took hold of the cage and carried it away, shutting him in alone.

For days he wandered round the edge of his compound grunting and calling, his back turned to his bleak private world that contained nothing at all but his heap of leaves and straw and nothing to do. There was no one to romp with, no one to follow, no need to forage, no stream to dabble in, no tree to climb, no daily excursion in the rich covering forest, no possibility of disappearing from this pitiless exposure. He sat with his face pressed to the wire listening and longing, but he never heard his own language again or smelled the com-

fortable family aura. Such loneliness was not to be endured.

Often all day the camp was deserted, and then he exhausted himself in his efforts to get out, squealing for his mother. No wonder that when his captor's friend came back, when he came in to him and offered treats, Hanno grew to welcome him—to like it even when he was rolled over and tickled, when the man laughed when he laughed. If he grew suddenly resentful again and bit, he was cuffed, and he liked that too. The Old Man was a great cuffer. Anyway, it was far more interesting when someone was there than when he was alone. He made do with human company, but he did not forget. The red-faced hairy man called Blair he saw more rarely, and always spat at. Had Hanno but known it, this compound that he was so anxious to escape from—this patch of grass and stones shaded by a tree and surrounded by open bushes and the tantalizing edges of the forest, pressed upon by the heavily scented air and interrogated with parrot squawks by day and the laughter of hyenas at night, was the last he was ever to know of his heritage, the elemental earth. He looked at it for a month, and then was put back into a travelling cage and sent off on a long journey, by truck, by canoe, by truck again, by aeroplane, by train, by truck; shaken and deafened and hopeless and sick, faced only by strangers, till he was delivered more dead than alive into the kind and understanding hands of the keeper who was to be his only friend and his guardian for life.

Part Two

It was morning in the Monkey House—one of those bitterly cold May days with driving snow that sometimes happen in an English summer. Through the grubby glass roof the colourless London light filtered down, helped by electricity to something approaching the gaiety of the inside of King's Cross station. The wide floor between the two rows of cages had been newly scrubbed and was as inviting as wet concrete ever is.

Through the door came an army of children enjoying a school treat. They fought to enter, were squeezed into eager immobility in the doorway, arms and legs locked, and burst yelling into the interior. Among them was a Chinese boy known to his friends as Ping, though that was not his real name. He was an orphan refugee living in a hostel. He was trim, self-possessed and gay, and he thought his own thoughts. Indeed he was so unlike his companions both in race and circumstance that his thoughts would scarcely have been understood or welcomed. His firm tight little mouth gave way to curled smiles which were all the more attractive because of the impression that only half the smile had been allowed out. He came through the door in a squeezing mass with the others, who ran shouting and pointing down the rows of cages, laughing and being peevishly answered back by the monkeys. Ping was no sooner inside than he was squirming with distaste. What had he in his innocence expected? A great pavilion full of palms, banana trees and giant ferns, streamers of orchids hanging down from the ceiling smelling of everything exotic, among which the monkeys peeped and sprang as gaily as at home? Before he had been displaced he had watched monkeys in his own forest as European children might watch squirrels in the New Forest, speckled with sun and shade, their bright eyes inquisitive and carefree. Certainly it had never occurred to him that an animal could be stripped of everything that went with it, of which its instincts were an inseparable part, and that you could have just its little body in a space of nothingness. As if looking at *that* told you anything but the nature of sorrow, which you knew anyway. Here in their ugly empty cages the monkeys were no more tropical than a collection of London rats or dirty park pigeons. They were degraded as in a slum. Some sat frowning with empty eyes, and those that wasted their unbelievable grace of movement in leaping from perch to chain, from chain to roof, from roof to perch to chain, repeating it for ever, had reduced to fidgety clockwork the limitless ballet of the trees which is vital joy.

Ping stood there saddened. He wanted to run out, but that was no good. What he really wanted was never to have come in. And then suddenly his attention was seized and he felt nothing but intense excitement. Ping had the kind of imagination that never dismisses anything as ordinary. Nothing was ordinary to him. What was always most surprising was just how extraordinary things are. It was hard to keep up with it. Now he saw in a special cage shut off from all the others, with a double row of bars between it and the public and plate glass round the outside as well, a stupendous black figure standing like a horse; like a horse that was also a man, for it had a man's brow and compelling authoritative eyes, but its nostrils were large and soft like a horse's. Suddenly it sprang round facing him and stood upright. It *was* a man! It was a giant with a bare black chest ten times as wide as Ping's own. He could see the breaths it took.

This creature turned its back and walked to the rear of its cage where there was a step to a raised platform and a low door. Its legs were short in comparison with its size but very powerful, while the muscles of its back and shoulders were something Ping looked at and knew he failed to imagine properly. It was too much. It laid a hand on the platform and vaulted effortlessly up, turning round in the all-fours position to face Ping. Its attitude was that of whirlwind force held ready and very lightly triggered. It was listening intently and turned its magnificent crested head in quick jerks from side to side. Ping dropped his eyes for a second to read the label on the cage. He could not wait any longer to know.

HANNO
GORILLA GORILLA. BELGIAN CONGO
AGED 13

Hanno took advantage of his raised position to hurl himself at the front of his cage. People scattered with cries of fright, but Ping gripped the rail, too rapt to move. Hanno's leaps were catapult-violent, but he landed in balance ready for another spring in any direction. After much leaping to and fro and up and down, and pressing his face to the bars in an effort to see further out sideways, while Ping stood just in front lost in admiration, Hanno walked across to a cast iron door leading to the Keeper's passage at one side of his cage. He tried it sharply to see if it was locked, as of course it was, and he knew that as well as anyone else. He then examined it all round the edge, prising and pushing with fingers as strong as tyre levers.

It would not budge. He flicked himself back against the opposite wall in a sidelong action of two legs and one arm, and turned to face the door. With a bound he was back upon it, standing erect to pound on the door with his fists. It was an expert smashing drum-roll, getting faster and faster, till he finished with both arms stylishly raised like a tympanist in a symphony who has just had his big moment, the final Boom! Boom! In this case CLANG CLANG. The Monkey House shook to the passionate gong. It was loud enough, one would have thought, to have halted the London traffic outside. Inside the chimpanzees began to imitate him, and to stamp and clap, and the other monkeys to scream.

The teacher was tugging at Ping's arm.

"We are going to the Lion House," she yelled. "Come along."

Ping shook his head, then as the noise died down for a moment he said, still gazing at Hanno, "I'm staying here." Just in time he remembered his manners, turning with the little bow he still did unconsciously, "Please".

The teacher had not bothered to look at Hanno—monkeys were for children, like Teddy Bears and Golliwogs, but she was beguiled by Ping's gravity and his air of determination. She could recognize when a child really was immovable except by force. So she said "Very well. Stay here and don't go anywhere else till I come back."

Ping hardly knew she had gone. Hanno was trying the second door, which led to his back yard. He leant against it and beat it with his elbow, for all the world like a man waiting for the pub door to open. His bangs this time were confidential, though still commanding; but in vain. Back he went to an assault on the Keeper's door, this time using his shoulder as a battering ram launched with all his force and weight across the width of the cage. What a creature to dare to imprison, not only physically to dare, but morally. What *was* shut up here?

Of all this monstrous commotion nobody came to take any notice. Ping could hardly suppose it happened every day. What if the door gave way?

At last Hanno tired and sat down. He sighed like a weary athlete and crossed his arms. Then he settled into a position of age-long patient impatience, just sitting. The very expression of his face was that of years of sitting. Ping had seen it in refugee camps. He knew that sort of thing. For the first time his attention strayed from the gorilla to focus on the cage where the prisoner yawned and rubbed his knuckles. It was smaller than he had thought. Hanno had made it look big simply because while looking at him the imagination could not contain him in so little space. The cage was just big enough for him to take a bound from corner to corner, or he could stretch to his full height on the platform and touch the ceiling. It was as if Ping were shut up for life in a bathroom. The walls were tiled and the floor concrete. He had a horror of concrete. It was one of his nightmares. He had lived on it in refugee camps that were often warehouses or railway sheds. That was where he had come to know and loathe it. It was either deathly cold or mercilessly hot and had a hateful feeling under one's fingers, like rust. Every time his hands or the soles of his feet came in contact with it, they remembered the warm boulders, the live turf, the leafy forest tracks, the tree trunks that you patted for pleasure and put an arm round without reasoning why. When all the country was your own. Ping's father had been a well-to-do timber merchant. They lived in the Burmese borderland in a fine wooden house on the edge of the forest, where Ping, who was an only child, played all

43

day long, watching the foresters or simply playing with his own imagination and the whole twinkling variety of the glades and brooks. And now he remembered acutely the day when he returned from the forest eager and hungry, to find his father's house and the little settlement round it burnt out and utterly deserted, with all the signs of violence and wanton desecration. He had run calling and calling among the charred logs and the desolate silence, till at last the little son of the steward crawled out of the pigsty where he was hiding, and told him "they" had been, looking for someone who was supposed to be hidden in his father's house, and those who had not been killed had been taken away. Who had been killed, he did not know, he had heard the guns but he was hiding all the time. Everyone had gone. The two children were afraid to stay near such a place. They had wandered away together, eating berries and mushrooms and nuts and begging in tiny villages. Sometimes they slept in deserted temples among the carved stone elephants and figures. In one of these, whose gateways and steps were mother of pearl and indigo in the moonlight and whose inner chambers were mysterious with looming faces and the shifting sounds of night, they found other children in the same plight. In the end it was a Buddhist monk who took them all to a Mission, where they were fed and passed on. From there the life on concrete began—concrete which seems to be chosen because where it is there can be nothing else—not the tiniest covering of lichen or moss, nor the slenderest blade of grass. The most it can tolerate is green or yellow slime. It is a kind of solid nothingness, it takes nothing in, it gives nothing back. On this unresponsive surface Hanno now sat, and could not even crumble it under his fingers. He had a pile of straw in one corner, but otherwise nothing, nothing at all. Here there was neither sunrise nor

His level eyes rested on Ping

sunset, mist or dew or the smell of changing seasons, nor change of any kind at all, but always his captive body with the primeval vitality that was the birthright of his great race, turning and turning upon itself in a few square yards of empty space. There was no breaking down his passion. For as long as Ping's lifetime he had been here unreconciled.

As if Ping had really been reading his thoughts, Hanno sprang into action again, hurling himself shoulder first against that door, thirty stone of weight behind each blow, then round his cage on all fours like a whirlwind again and again, as if he were tightening a coil, till at last he stood erect in the centre. Reaching to his full height, his arms above his head with clasped hands tense and superb, he began slowly circling round in a tragic dance. Ping's heart stopped beating. Never had he seen any gesture so proud and so despairing. It was like Samson praying for strength to pull the place down. Ping looked round, needing some other human to have seen this with him. The Monkey House was momentarily empty. He and Hanno must have it as a secret between them.

Hanno had sat down again and was winding straw between his fingers. Now and again his level eyes, chestnut where the light caught them, rested on Ping.

"Hanno," he said in his gentlest voice. For Ping had, as it were, fallen in love. The world contained something so wonderful to him that everything was altered. It was not only that Hanno existed, a creature with the strength of a bull, the agility of a spider, the pounce of a lion, the sensitivity of a horse and the dignity and grief of a man—too much to take in, all the animal creation in one—but somewhere there was a country of such size, power and mystery that gorillas were a sample of what it produced in secret, where everything else would be on the same scale. The world always had surprises, and between every surprise there were other surprises. There was no end to what might be. Something like this Ping felt without words, losing all sense of time, while people of all kinds drifted past the cages.

"That's an ugly great brute to meet in the dark," they said. They said it one after the other in procession, each as if it were an original remark. Only the tiniest children looked at Hanno without prejudice, and an infant in arms said "Dad-dad" amid shrieks of laughter. Ping stood his ground while crowds formed and melted away.

"Coo! Aint 'e awful."

"Oh look, darling, a gorilla. Isn't he a horrid big thing."

An affected voice said in a whisper:

"Look, Humphrey. Did you ever see such a *peach*." Ping looked round to see who could be going so far wrong in the other direction. An over-smart lady beamed condescendingly at him, and dipping suddenly into her shopping bag pulled out a peach which she pressed into his hand. Before he could speak she waved coyly and moved on. Peach in hand he turned back to his magnet.

An under-keeper came along with a tray of mugs which he was taking to the young chimpanzees farther down the row.

"Is this one dangerous?" somebody asked pointing at Hanno.

"Nasty great brute. Never trust him an inch." The under-keeper edged into the passage with his tray. "He'll get you if he can. Just waiting his chance."

The crowds hurried after him to watch the chimpanzees being fed. He went in to them, gave them a mug each and taught them table manners. They were amusing caricatures of ugly children. They did not wear about them the grandeur of their place of origin. Perhaps they came of a long line of

47

chimpanzees born in captivity and now as nondescript as the sparrows that hopped in and out of their cages.

Ping went back to Hanno, who was quivering and making soft muzzle grunts, his eyes blazing like a lover's under his heavy brows. Quietly and suddenly the Head Keeper was there, unlocking the intermediate door into the space between the double set of bars, which formed a narrow corridor between the public and the cages. He carried a large enamel jug and a bucket of cooked potatoes. He was a man who did not need to assert authority. It was his by nature. He inspired confidence in animals and men, and both knew at sight that it would never be abused. As he moved in close to the bars, Hanno sprang at them with a snarling bark, pressing himself against them.

"You naughty boy," said the Keeper surprisingly, unmoved by the charge. "Is that the way you greet me when I come back? Behave yourself, you bad boy." Ping remembered that Hanno was only thirteen. "He's like some people," the Keeper went on chattily to the bystanders. "If they want you to come and you don't come, when you do come the first word they say isn't a welcome. It's a curse."

Hanno now squatted in the friendliest way, sticking two fingers through the bars as far as the very narrow space would allow, and also his long horse's underlip which was pinched by the bars into the shape of a jug. Into this the Keeper poured condensed milk and eggs. Hanno's finger-tips pushed at the sides of the jug to get possession of it.

"Put your hands down, you bad boy."

He laid them obediently in his lap. The Keeper scratched him lovingly under the chin, and said kind words to him. He scraped the sticky bottom of the jug with his fingers and gave them to Hanno to suck.

48

"He has been waiting for you a long time," said Ping.

"I know he has. I've been away sick for a fortnight."

"Who looks after him then?"

"Why, my second in command. But Hanno understands me better, because I brought him up from a baby."

"Do you groom him every day? He looks so clean. He looks in his best clothes."

"He keeps himself like that, with his straw."

"But do you go inside with him?"

"I could. I'd be all right with him. I used to go in every day, to romp with him. When you go in with them, you must never look at them or seem to take any notice. Just pretend you are about your own business, sweeping perhaps, or just sitting reading the paper. After a time they will come of their own accord and sit near you for company. He was a baby when he came. I went in with him every day till he was nearly as big as he is now. A terrible rough weight he was to romp with. Used to knock the wind out of me. Then one day he decided we ought to stay together—either he came out with me or I stayed there with him. You can imagine if he puts those arms of his round you, there isn't much you can do against him. I had to get the other keepers to help me out. Since then I never go in."

"How did they get you out?"

"They had to trick him into it. Nobody can make him do anything he doesn't want to. He's not like the chimps and the orang-utans—you can make them do anything. But if you want him to do something, you've got to be cleverer than he is. You have to pretend you don't want him to do it. Make as if you want to shut his inner door, and he'll be through in a flash."

The Keeper was handing potatoes in their jackets to Hanno

one by one. The thick black fingers pushing through to take them were anything but clumsy. They juggled everything expertly through.

"You have to watch out," he went on as if he were training Ping for the post of under-keeper. "Those fingers are strong enough to pull your hand through and snap your arm between the bars. He wouldn't mean to. He's just too strong." The Keeper didn't seem to be watching out, or anything, but relaxed and quietly at home with a friend, but doubtless he missed nothing, and Hanno certainly was watching him. Although his eyes were as straight as a man's and deeply set in overhanging sockets, he seemed able to see sideways.

"You see how he watches without moving his head. That's instinctive, because in the forest it's movement that betrays you, but moving eyes would only be like glittering leaves. In the forest you never know if there isn't one close beside you. You neither hear them nor see them. While you are trailing them, they may be trailing you."

"He tries all the time to get out," said Ping. "What if the iron bars were rusted?"

The Keeper laughed at his ignorance.

"Those aren't *iron*," he made it sound the most rubbishy material. "Those are steel. If it was iron, he'd pull them apart as easy as a child playing bows and arrows, and walk right out."

"What if the lock of the door gave way?"

"I've thought of that too, young man. There is a padlock, and a special catch on the lock in case he should find a bit of a stick in his straw stiff enough to pick the lock with. He's quite capable of that. And there are spikes on the upper half of the door, see, to stop him battering it down. No door could take the kind of battering he gives it. He did crack the hinges before we put in those spikes."

"He has been charging it with his shoulder," said Ping.

"Maybe. But not how he could do."

Not how he could do! What more could be imagined?

Hanno all this while was delicately peeling potatoes and throwing the skin on the floor. He carefully brushed off any bits that fell on himself. Ping became aware of the warm velvet skin of the peach that he was still holding between his hands.

"Can I give this to him?"

"You can give it to me, and I'll give it to him from you." He came out from his corridor and took the peach. A little crowd had gathered again to watch. The Keeper showed it to Hanno, whose willing fingers came through and twitched. "This is for you, Hanno, from that young gentleman there," he said, pointing to Ping who felt immensely proud. The peach was dropped into Hanno's fingers, two only of each hand, and he coaxed it delicately through, sniffed it deeply and stuffed it into his mouth. It was gone in one glorious glubbery squelch of cheek and tongue. He spat out the stone.

"Did he know it was from me?"

"Of course he did. Didn't you see how he smelled your fingers? He won't forget you. He has a lot of friends, only none of them bring him peaches. But you needn't expect him to be grateful."

Ping's modesty had not imagined any such thing. "I suppose you're his best friend," he said enviously, thinking of Oskar, who was his.

"It doesn't do to flatter yourself. I don't have to get sentimental. He's a big dominating chap. We know each other well and it's an armed neutrality. He's well looked after, but maybe he has other ideas. It's the Welfare State here, they are better off than they know. He wouldn't have all that bounce if he wasn't happy."

"He does bounce, like a ball. I can't think how he does it."

"Ah, he's all right where he is. The African forest's not so good, you know. It's full of horrors."

"That's why he is what he is," thought Ping, but he only said regretfully, "I don't know when I can come again."

"Never mind. Hanno's got a long memory. He'll remember that peach. Well, I must be getting on. Good-bye young man."

"Thank you," said Ping, smiling all joy.

A gentleman who was standing by caught the Keeper's eye.

"I am interested in the different ways he has of expressing himself. He seems to have a lot to say. Is there ever anything that could be a word?"

"Not words. But grunts, sniffs, snorts, expletives, chuckles, spits. A lot of men hardly use more. He uses a variety of throat sounds as well, which are changing all the time as he grows up. Lately, first thing in the morning, he has begun making a kind of sobbing, birdlike call. I don't know what it means, unless he's lonely. It might be a mating call."

"In the wild I suppose they are very ferocious?"

"No, sir. That's a false idea. They only want to be left alone. If you don't interfere with them they won't interfere with you. They are quiet vegetarians. Of course here he's like a dog in a cage. He can swear blue murder at everyone because he knows he can't get at them or they at him. He's showing off. Anyway a caged animal can't be normal. You never know what they'll do."

"Has he in fact ever hurt anyone?"

"Once he clawed someone. Some fools will have it, you know. I couldn't blame Hanno."

"It must take a lot of food to fill him."

"You'd be surprised. Enough vegetables and fruit to keep five families. About twenty pounds weight a day. Good day, sir. Excuse me."

Hanno now seemed pacified. He took his bundle of straw and shook the potato skins out of it, putting the straw on the platform. Then he picked all the bits up and threw them out of the cage, even deliberately and contemptuously at the spectators, whom he could not hit because of the glass in between. He went back for his straw, fluffed it up well and sat down in it, looking at the crowd as if he had just made an entrance and was sitting in judgement on them. He took a fistful of straw and put it on his head; found by accident among it a piece of bass string about two feet long, which he took some trouble to arrange over the top of his straw wig so that an end hung evenly down to each shoulder. It suggested a Pharaoh's head-dress. So ceremoniously crowned, he looked like the chief of chiefs, and nobody was inclined to laugh.

The school children were all there again, dragging their feet a little now. The mistress said, "Come along, Ping. You've missed a great deal, hasn't he children? But I'm glad you are still here. We were much longer than I expected because we lost our way. Did you think we were never coming?"

"No," said Ping following quietly. "I was with Hanno. And the Keeper," he added as no one seemed to know what he meant. On the way out he passed Hanno's outside yard—a small square of concrete with a glass wind shelter at one end.

They went on to the Tower—another prison where long ago people who were never to come out had scratched their names on the walls.

In the Underground going back to their distant suburb, the children roared like lions, barked like sea-lions, paced about like tigers, scratched each others' shoulders like monkeys and flapped like cranes: it was a pandemonium that the teacher was unable to control. The other passengers however rather enjoyed it. It was infectious. The children were all going homeward. Only Ping was going instead to the International Relief Society's Intermediate Hostel for Displaced Children. It was in one of the buildings belonging to a disused airfield, with vistas of concrete inside and out. Over the entrance was a semicircle of buttercup yellow letters, THE FUTURE IS YOURS. As Ping had been passed from camp to camp for five years, starting in Singapore, he spoke good English and went to the local school. Some of the children in the hostel were newcomers and spoke little English yet. Some of them could speak to nobody. His own special friend Oskar had been found a home with a family in Canada. They had gone to school together and Ping missed him very much. They had also had last year a wonderful holiday together. After seeing Hanno the memory of those fabulously free early morning or moonlight hours on the river at Green Knowe was very much on his mind. Would it ever happen again? Oskar was gone, but Ping had one other special friend, the girl called Ida who was the third on that adventure. She sometimes wrote to Ping, who was in fact, though he was too reserved to know it, a general favourite. He took everything in his stride, and if he did not like what was there he called upon his fancy to supply him with something more entertaining. However, his meeting with Hanno had left him feeling troubled, excited and bewildered, a very small person with long, long thoughts and the very oddest hero-worship.

That night he dreamed he was back in his father's forest. It was of fantastic beauty. The setting sun poured fire through it along the ground, lighting up the emerald mounds of moss, the fan-vaulting of the trees and the smooth boulders like men lying asleep and breathing. The violet shadows that soon would come down from the trees like a curtain were being held upward till the sun's arm should drop. Only the boles of the trees made purple bars along the ground, where a tiger was lying on its back happily boxing at a twig that was tickling it. Ping was pleased that it was there.

At breakfast he sat among twenty lost children eating porridge. No one talks much in exile, and children who are uncertain are as silent as blocks however hard the grown-ups try. Ping was making a porridge island in the middle of his plate with a milk sea. The sea was too full of rocks for any ship to cross it, the island too thick with trees for any aeroplane to land. Under the trees.... The little boy sitting next to him was doing as he did, with a look of serious questioning and content.

"There's a letter here for you, Ping," said the Warden who was sorting through a handful. "You may read it after breakfast." Ping was the only one who ever had a letter. The other children all looked at him as at someone very grand. Ida's letter lay beside his plate and radiated happiness into his face.

Dear Ping, [she had written].

I have been for a ride on the carrier of Aunt Maud's motorbike. It was very bumpy. She had finished her book. There was a photo of Terak's tooth in it and pages of stupid talk and long words. I asked her if she was going to Green Knowe again this summer, but she said No, it wasn't to let. I was thinking perhaps you and I might be invited. It is a shame Oskar has gone. We did have a wonderful time. Then I

thought you might come with us, but Mother says we have
to have a crowd of stupid cousins and there won't be room.
So I asked Aunt Maud couldn't she write to Mrs. Thing who
lives at Green Knowe and ask if you could go there to her.
Aunt Maud said you couldn't do things like that. We don't
know Mrs. Oldknow. But I thought, if we don't know her,
we don't know if we could or not. So I wrote to her myself,
and said we loved Green Knowe particularly *for reasons*, and
could she possibly ask you because Oskar had gone. I thought
you would like it even if you were alone. And you could
write and tell me everything, because I should wish like
anything that I was there too.

Love from

IDA

PS. I did the envelope very specially so that she would not
miss it. I hope it works.

Ping went off to school as lively as a trout in a stream. The
world was full of surprises and possibilities. So long as you
weren't in a cage.

Part Three

I

Ida's scheme worked. The old lady who lived in the enchanted house at Green Knowe on the day she received Ida's letter had had a disappointment. Her favourite great-grandson, Tolly, who usually spent his holidays with her, was to spend the summer with his father who was coming home on leave from Burma. She had hoped they would all stay with her, but Tolly's stepmother had chosen to go to Scotland. After she had read the letter announcing this, Mrs. Oldknow laid it down and did not feel much interest in the other envelopes waiting for her attention. "Oh bother that woman!"

57

she said, taking off her glasses and wiping them slowly. "I *enjoy* Tolly's company." She laid her glasses down on a childish-looking envelope. Through the lenses the writing was magnified. It also stood up off the paper. The words Green Knowe struck her as having been written with more than care. There was something about them that suggested that to the writer they were words of magic importance. Was it just the way they were placed in the exact centre of the envelope? She put on her glasses again and picked up the letter. Each corner was decorated with a little drawing. In the top left hand was a horse with wings, in the top right of course the stamp, bottom left a windmill, and bottom right a man wearing stag's antlers. Wavy lines done over the watermark framed the address as if it were on an island. It was neatly and beautifully done.

Mrs. Oldknow looked at it and smiled. Men with antlers are magic all the world over. So are flying horses. What about windmills? Potentially they could mean many things, but nothing special to her. She opened the letter with considerable curiosity.

Ida had tried to be as correct and grown up as possible in the wording. Only on the envelope she had given way to special treatment, lest the stiff unnatural sentences inside should be too weak for their purpose. The ending had given her a lot of trouble:

... I am sure if you gave him a trial you would find Ping nice company, and he hardly eats anything. He is a year and a half younger than me but quite old for his age.

Thanking you in anticipation,

Yours sincerely,
IDA BIGGIN

Mrs. Oldknow laughed aloud. "That seems settled, then," she said to herself as there was no one else to say it to. "I can't have Tolly, but I shall have Ping."

She was so old and had lived in Green Knowe so long, that she had come to accept quietly whatever curious things presented themselves there, and almost to think it was the house itself which made things happen. These children, Ida, Oskar and Ping, had come to Green Knowe the year before, when she herself was away, but the house had caught hold of them and was pulling them back. For Green Knowe was not like any other house. It was of such antiquity that its still being there was hardly believable. By all the rules of time and change it should long long ago have become a ruined heap of stone, the sort of place that haunts the imagination because there is only just enough of it to start you off—one window upstairs in a single wall, or a broken threshold among the nettles. Somehow, century after century while much younger castles and houses rotted or were burnt down, or their owners grew tired of them and cleared them away to make room for new, Green Knowe stood quietly inside its moat and its belt of trees. Its stone was crumbling a little, its roof sagged between the rafters till they showed like the ribs of an old horse. A feeling of love and enchantment settled down on it, distilled out of all the sunrises and sunsets, moonrises and moonsets and tilting constellations that went over it, as each day added to its already legendary existence. And when the very walls of the house you live in are almost impossible to believe in, you are not likely to question the probability of the things that happen there. "For every person who comes here," Mrs. Oldknow reflected, "different things happen. Ping who comes from so far away, will certainly bring quite other adventures. The girl Ida said in her letter they loved Green Knowe *for reasons*. I

59

don't suppose Ping will tell me what those adventures were. As usual I shall have to guess. But that's an exercise that I enjoy."

She wrote at once to the International Relief Society's Intermediate Hostel for Displaced Children, inviting Ping for the summer holidays.

Ping's journey was long enough to be interesting but not so difficult as to be an ordeal. He enjoyed his independence, and nobody watching him hop in and out of trains would have guessed how exciting and privileged an occasion it was for him. He had much to think about too, as he left London behind him. He was not the only one for whom a door had unexpectedly opened. Freedom was in the air. The passenger in the far corner opposite was reading the paper, holding it up in front of his face so that Ping could read the outside sheets.

NOT NICE TO MEET ON A DARK NIGHT

in huge black type from side to side. And underneath was a photo, crumpled by the man's fingers, but which was certainly Hanno, shaking his bars. Beside the photo smaller headlines read: *Gorilla Escapes from Zoo. Police alerted.* Ping read this till it seemed printed on his eyeballs, but before he could read further, the reader folded over the page and became so interested in something else that Ping never had a chance to read more about Hanno. He felt immensely elated. For the first time for ten years Hanno had sprung farther than the width of his cage. Surely he would burst right out. He would not hide in the keepers' underground passages or the stoke holes. He would avoid all buildings in future. But outside, in the great asphalted Zoo, or the macadamed yellow-lit roads, there was no place for him. Ping asked himself what he would do in that position. He imagined Hanno climbing over the top of the lions' cages, perhaps if he were hard-pressed, pulling the bars apart and letting them out too, to complicate the chase. Would lions have steel bars, or not having hands to pull with, would iron do? Would Hanno let everything else out as he went past? And then what? He wriggled with joy at the thought of the square and shaggy black form darting about in the night, drumming on walls to drive the animals out, standing upright flattened against corners to watch and listen. "Police alerted". What were the police supposed to do? Hanno wearing the Keeper's hat and crossing the road among the crowd behind the policeman's outstretched arm, exchanging the Keeper's hat for a policeman's helmet and truncheon. Whacko, so much for the police. He knew all this was crazy cinema fantasy, but he wished with all his heart that Hanno could get right away.

Other passengers got in with different papers.

EMPTY, REGENT'S PARK CORDONED OFF.

MYSTERY AT THE ZOO, KEEPER FINDS GORILLA'S CAGE

Another had a portrait of Hanno with his most calculating human expression and the words:

WANTED. £2,000 WORTH OF MURDEROUS MUSCLE AT LARGE. People living in the neighbourhood of Regent's Park are warned to be careful. Every effort is being made to catch this valuable beast alive. The Keeper is certain he will have made for the Park, where, inside a cordon of police reinforced by commandos, the Zoo van is circling in readiness. The Head Keeper who is exposing himself to all risks, hopes to coax his savage ex-playmate into it, or tempt him with drugged food. Instructions have been given to the police and troops that the animal is not to be shot unless he has successfuly broken through the cordon. The public is advised that the animal will probably not attack unless he is provoked and is certain to avoid houses. All the same, residents near the Park are warned—if you have a shrubbery watch it. And keep your dog on the lead.

Ping watched and waited, reading what he could between the fingers of the holder, teased when the page was turned too soon, screwing his head on one side to read papers that lay at right-angles on the seat, but too polite to ask for one.

Out of the window he summed up every hedge or spinney from the point of view of Hanno's hiding there. But of course he was leaving all that behind him. He pictured the squandering spread of brick, stone, concrete, glass, metal, tarmac, pavement, railings and dank courtyards that made up London. Hanno hadn't a chance. He was probably already trapped.

Penny Soaky! Penny Soaky! shouted the porter. At the station and in the taxi going to Green Knowe, Ping was suddenly afraid he was going to miss Ida and Oskar too much to enjoy anything. At each turn of the view the words Do you remember? came to his lips, but there was no one to say them to. However, when the little old lady opened the door, with her fine gay wrinkles moving in welcome, his first thought was—she's like a Chinese old lady and he felt at home. He gave the bow he would have given to his own grandmother.

"I am very glad you could come, Ping. My Tolly is away and he has taken his dog with him. And Mr. Boggis the gardener is away too on his holidays, so I should have been quite alone if you hadn't come. It's very nice for me, and I hope it won't be dull for you. You know the house already so you should feel quite at home."

"It's different this time," he said, looking round the living-room with astonished affection. A transformation had taken place since the real owner had returned. The whole house smelled of flowers, and there was a litter of things for living with and looking at, where before it had been bare.

"How is it different?" she asked surprised.

He thought this over carefully.

"The furniture looks in the right place. When Dr. Biggin was here it looked pushed about, and . . . intermediate."

"Intermediate? You mean like a hostel? Oh Ping! You put your finger right on my guilty conscience. When people let their houses, they lock up their nicest things in an empty room and put out instead the second and third best, the things that will 'do'. I hope I didn't overdo it. I wasn't expecting you! What a good thing you came again to give me a second chance."

"We loved it. But wouldn't Ida be surprised if she saw it now! I've never been in a house where somebody really lived—I mean not since I grew up. I do remember my father's house, but I've been displaced since I was six."

"So you grew up when you were six? Ida said you were quite old for your age."

"You grow up when you leave home, don't you," said Ping confidingly as between equals.

"What was your home like?"

"It was a big wooden house with steps up to it, and the roof tree stuck out at each end, turned up like the prow of a boat, and painted." Ping made a gesture with both of his arms to show how it went. "And there was forest all round it. And a river for floating logs down."

"I am sorry there is no forest for you here. But there is quite a nice wood beyond the moat, called Toseland Thicket. But of course you know that."

"Yes, I know there is a wood there. But we couldn't see it out of the bedroom windows, we saw the river, and the river always gave Ida so many ideas that we rushed off to the canoe every day. We never went into the wood at all, not once. How could we bear not to?"

"It's not really odd. When three people are together they do quite different things from what one person does alone. So you slept in the attic? I have put you there again. It is Tolly's room really, but yours to you. I have put a big Chinese lantern outside your door to light you up at night. Can you take your case up? Then wash your hands and come down to tea."

Ping was pleased to be in the attic bedroom again. His bed was there, and Oskar's, but Ida's camp-bed had been taken out. He leaned out of the window and looked at the river, remembering everything that had happened a year ago and smiling at the thought of it. Already he knew that this time everything was going to be quite different, but not less interesting. He looked at the huge Chinese lantern outside the bedroom door, put there to welcome him. It was nearly as big as himself, and when he switched on the light inside it, it looked like sunshine through bamboo leaves. It hung in a little enclosed place at the top of the stairs, low enough to shine on Ping's face as he stood admiring it. But Ping could not see how much more at home the lantern looked because of him beside it.

There was more welcome waiting for him. When he sat down to tea he stared at the cup in front of him, and then at Mrs. Oldknow, and back at the china, as if he were trying hard to wake up, and his food remained on his plate.

"What's the matter, Ping? Aren't you hungry?"

"It's the cups," he said.

It looked like sunshine through bamboo leaves.

E

They were thin blue cups without handles, patterned with glazed oval windows the size of rice grains, through which the light shone when they were held up. "At first I just felt queer and happy and didn't know why. But now I feel sure. My mother had those cups at home when I was little. I'm sure I'm not dreaming."

He put his hand out and touched the china. "How do you come to have so many things?"

"It's the house," she said. "It always seems to be by accident. But when you, for instance, come here out of the blue, look at all the things that are waiting specially for you— for I'm sure you'll find others—for you and nobody else. These are quite ordinary Chinese cups. Everybody notices them, because of their windows, but for you they are your mother's."

Afterwards they went into the garden, into the hidden part at the back of the house. Here there was a big lawn that was so encircled with trees, walls and shrubberies as to be invisible except from an aeroplane. Even from the house only tempting glimpses could be seen through the trees. The flower-beds were designed in a pattern, but not strictly. The patterns led to escapes, to odd corners, to unexpected walks, to special exhilarating smells, and to the shady edge of the surrounding moat, once a branch of the river. On the far side the water was overhung by a dense belt of bamboo, and behind that lay Toseland Thicket.

"We never came in this part of the garden last year," said Ping. "Miss Bun said children spelled ruination to gardens, and we were to keep to the front. You can't even see this properly from the house, from any of the windows. I used to try. And from the front no one would know it was here."

"Did you really never see it? What a waste."

"Never. Not even by moonlight."

Something about the way he said moonlight made her think of Ida's men with antlers, but she didn't know why. "Did you often go out by moonlight?"

"Oh yes."

"Well you can come here as much as you like now, moonlight or sunlight. It's quite true that children are hard on gardens. But so are birds. On the other hand, it's children and birds that enjoy gardens most. Look at them now."

The garden was full of them, all sizes and colours, very tame, watching what was going on and playing in and out of the paths, hedges and bushes as if the whole place had been laid out for them.

"Does nobody ever come here but you?"

"Very seldom. Visitors sometimes. The gardener of course, but he's away now. And this isn't the part of the garden he likes. He likes his gardens tidy with their hair cut. I like them what the gardening books call rampant, that is to say rollicking all over the place if they want to. So we divide the garden in two and each have half as we like it."

They went round together. Ping ran off here and there to see where everything went to, returning out of breath to his hostess like a laughing and expectant dog. As they approached the house again they came face to face with the old stone figure of St. Christopher that marked the entrance of a chapel that once stood there, having survived the chapel by four hundred years.

"I would like that by moonlight," said Ping. "I like it now, all wrapped up in jungle."

"How odd to hear our innocent English ivy and traveller's joy called jungle. Does he remind you of something too, that you look at him so lovingly?"

67

"Yes. Of half-ruined temples in the forest where Ho and I used to sleep. Inside, in the dark, there were things moving that might be monkeys, or might be snakes, or just creatures we don't know about who live in the dark. We always hoped it wasn't tigers or murderers, because the stone figures in the courtyard were supposed to keep evil things away. We were only very little boys."

"What a headful of thoughts and memories you have brought here," she said smiling. "I have a theory that events follow ideas. I mean ordinary things happen to ordinary people, but to some people only extraordinary things happen. That's why I love to have children here, because to them nothing is ordinary."

"Can we listen to the six o'clock news?" said Ping, very doubtful if it was polite to ask, but driven by his need to know.

"Now what can you be so specially interested in? Climbing the Himalayas? Rockets to the moon?"

"It's the escaped gorilla."

"What! Has a gorilla escaped? That, certainly, is exciting. Let's go in, it's just time."

"Hanno, the gorilla is still at large. It is now known how the escape took place. This is the Head Keeper's account. The animal has an inner and an outer cage, the communicating door worked from outside by a lever. He sleeps indoors but goes outside every morning and is shut out while the indoor cage is cleaned. It is an absolute rule in the Zoo that every cage even when empty is kept locked, for which every keeper carries a key. One of the under-keepers who had just cleaned Hanno's indoor cage was in the act of locking it when he received a message to go and help the Head Keeper and the Vet. who were having difficulty with a patient. He hurried off, apparently without

68

having turned the key. As it was a fine day, it was not until evening that another keeper opened the lever door to admit the gorilla to his inner cage, omitting to check that the door of this was locked. Because, as he said in his confession, if there was one cage no one would forget to lock, it's Hanno's. The surprising thing about the story is that Hanno did not escape till dark. The Head Keeper visits every animal before locking up time to see that all are settled. He says Hanno had made his bed as usual and was covered with straw, but he noticed an open eye shining in it, and spoke to him. He is now of the opinion that the gorilla was coolly waiting his time, knowing quite well that the door wasn't locked. His hearing is acute and he is very lock-conscious. The Keeper locked the Monkey House and went home. When Hanno came out, he must have closed his cage door behind him. The night-watchman heard nothing. Hanno had all night to get clear. The broken lock of the swing door into the Monkey House was the first thing to be noticed in the morning, and that was presumed to have been done from outside—some hooligan's lark. Hanno, the Zoo's greatest treasure, is always the first to be visited when the Head Keeper arrives. His door was shut, but his fluffed-up mound of straw attracted suspicion. There was no one under it. The emergency siren was sounded and the Head Keeper of each department warned on the inter-com. to search his district. Within an hour it was clear that the gorilla was not in the Zoo. He is presumed to be in the Park. Volunteers with experience of big-game hunting are asked to report to the Zoological Society in Regent's Park where the police in charge of protective operations have been allowed to set up temporary headquarters. For the satisfaction of public opinion the two under-keepers have been dismissed. I wouldn't dismiss them myself, said the Head Keeper. They'll have learnt their lesson. And it's not everyone who is willing to look after dangerous animals. And Hanno has his likes and dislikes, like everyone else. The public is informed that the idea is to locate the animal, but above all to avoid disturbing him and to contain him from a discreet distance until his Keeper can get there with doped bait and a mobile cage. Regent's Park is cordoned off. There will be no performance at the Open Air Theatre. Traffic is circulating as usual, as it is hoped this will tend to keep the gorilla in cover. The police are discouraging the public from hanging around. You might get in the way, and you might get hurt, they say. It's not just a monkey, it's a GORILLA."

Ping, while listening, was immobile with excitement. As soon as it was over he found it impossible to keep still. "I wish they didn't have to find him. I wish they didn't. Only I don't see where he can go."

Mrs. Oldknow looked at him with appreciation. "Do you mind so much?"

"I've seen him," said Ping as if that explained everything.

"What's he like?"

Ping was tongue-tied. What was Hanno like? At last he said "He's like a thunderstorm. A thunderstorm in a bottle. A Genie." Then he laughed. "He's out," he said.

"He was certainly born and bred in the world's most tremendous thunderstorms, crash bang every night till the earth rocks."

"He's got the arms for throwing lightning," said Ping. "I wish he didn't have to be caught."

"He sounds quite dangerous."

"He has his likes and dislikes. But the Keeper isn't afraid of him. They love each other. The Keeper says they don't, but I can see they do."

"Then perhaps he'll just go home, like a dog that's been out on a spree, guilty but glad."

"Hanno wouldn't be guilty. He's very proud."

"He might be glad to be safe and warm and well fed."

"No," said Ping softly, "he's prouder than that."

"You make me want to see him."

"What would you do if you found him in your hidden garden?"

"I don't know, Ping. I've never expected to meet one."

"Would you give him away?"

This was obviously a real question to Ping, not just how-would-it-be. Mrs. Oldknow considered and tried to imagine the situation. "Well, do you know, if he seemed to be enjoying it and not wanting to pull anyone's head off, I almost think I should put it off as long as possible. But it would be wrong, you know. People would be very angry."

"The garden's too small," said Ping with a sigh, "nothing is big enough."

"Why is it that the gorilla has taken your fancy so much? The orang-utan is the Asiatic ape. Didn't you look at him?"

"Yes. He's just a great big hairy pig-spider sunk into a nasty heap. He's given up."

"But the baby orangs are intelligent and amusing?"

"I know. But they'll grow up like him."

"Poor dears! At home they live in the tops of trees and rock in the sky and sing. I can't imagine what it sounds like. They don't like London."

"Hanno doesn't either. But he hasn't given up. He's the Big Black Boss. And he's out."

"I expect all the boys in England are glad. It's much better than the Man from Mars."

"I wonder if Ida's glad. May I write to her? But I think I'll

71

wait till tomorrow and then there will be more to say. Isn't it nice to have someone to talk to?"

"Haven't you anyone at the Hostel to talk to?"

"I used to have Oskar. But a lot of the children can't talk English yet. As soon as they can they go to homes. But everyone asks for Hungarians. May we go and look at the wood before it gets dark?"

Toseland Thicket was large, extending outwards from the boundaries of Green Knowe in the shape of an open fan. The near side was bounded by the moat. Even if there had been a boat to cross in, there was no possible path through the close-growing bamboo canes along the water's edge. Ping and Mrs. Oldknow walked in the fields round the outer boundary, which was a bramble hedge ten feet high and much thicker, looped over thorn bushes.

"The Thicket is my bird sanctuary," she said. "Even the most passionate egg collector would stick at this hedge. The only gate is inside the garden, and the only track something less than a rabbit track where I go every spring to a boggy place where there are oxlips."

It was one of those warm summer evenings when the sun does not sink huge and scarlet but drops languidly into a silvery feather bed piled high up into the West, so that dusk instead of growing fiery turns duck-egg blue and lingers as long as possible.

"If you want to go into the wood, you can, as it is not nesting time. Carefully, of course. I'll leave you at the gate, but don't be too long. It's bedtime. There are the starlings coming in to roost."

The air was full of them, chattering like a school treat coming home, alighting all together on one tree till they weighed it down, and then with a whoosh! taking off and settling in another, or swooping round the sky in coils made up of thousands of tiny rigid planes. Ping took a step or two into the wood. Already it was full of shadows. The trees were unnaturally still as though they had frozen into those bent or upright attitudes because he was looking at them, and would relax if he turned away. The starlings settled at last in the farther side of the Thicket. Night could be felt as something that was there, though not yet revealed. Ping felt his way in among the enclosing, nudging, clutching bushes but there literally was no path. While he was trying to free himself from a bramble that tugged at his coat, he caught his foot in a rope of ivy and fell sideways. It didn't make much noise as he only fell into a cushion of ivy, but the starlings at the other end of the wood took off again with a shrill explosion of voices, that clearly said "Fly! fly!" as a black cloud of birds wheeled off into the sky. It was a sound so urgent that Ping felt included in it, not as if he were the cause of it. The starlings were warning everything in the wood. About him, Ping? He smiled, and as he looked up through the branches at the agitated birds, he saw the evening star in a hyacinth-blue sky. He withdrew from the Thicket as quietly as a ghost. He was very happy and rather tired. He thought with pleasure of the attic where he was to sleep, with the sound of the water gate all night and the wide river views he would wake up to every morning. The starlings were behaving as though their bedroom was on fire and where could they sleep? Dark and owls were coming and they must get in somewhere. They flew from tree to tree.

"You've been upsetting the starlings," said Mrs. Oldknow smiling. "I have often wondered how many times a night one would have to disturb them before they went somewhere else. I should like to get rid of them, but I am nothing like so persistent as they are."

"I wasn't really anywhere near them," said Ping. "They are very touchy. I came away, but they haven't gone back."

When Mrs. Oldknow came up to say good night to Ping, when he was in bed, everything was quiet except for the young owls trying out their breaking voices.

"The starlings are squashed into two big elms covered with ivy," she said. "It was a very quarrelsome and discontented business. I wonder if poachers ever go in the wood. Did you see or hear anyone?"

"No," said Ping. "There wasn't anything there, except what woods have. There was a lot of that."

At breakfast time Mrs. Oldknow and Ping opened the newspaper together with almost equal interest. There was a photo of the Head Keeper, and another of floodlighting round the most likely parts of the Park, intended to discourage Hanno from breaking cover during the night when search would be too dangerous. They read the following article:

There is still no sign of Hanno the gorilla who escaped two nights ago from the Zoo. A party of six hand-picked men under the Head Keeper are continuing the search in Regent's Park, within the outer cordon of Police and Commandos. During the night when search was impossible police cars circulated constantly in the hope of containing the animal wherever he may be. A police dog on the leash was used at first, and after considerable delay because the gorilla was not always on the ground, led to the discovery of the first foot and knuckle marks in the loose soil of a covert. The sooty colour of the animal would help to con-

74

ceal him. From this point the presence of the dog was considered more of a danger than a help. The gorilla seems to have spent some time in the Open Air Theatre, and gone from there to the Queen's Garden. The tracks double and criss-cross. The search of course took time to organize and in any case has to be a slow and cautious business with the Zoo van at hand. The party contains two experienced big-game hunters. The whole of Regent's Park was covered yesterday, but the search continues in case the gorilla slipped back to parts already searched. Every tree is suspect. Our special correspondent had an interview with the Keeper who says that there has been no sign of Hanno in the Zoo itself, where the most probable place would be one of the food stores. He is a voracious eater, requiring twenty pounds of vegetables and fruit a day. Hunger must bring him out. He may even return of his own accord to his cage which is standing open with food inside. The Zoo remains closed to the public. The gorilla is by nature shy and an expert in hiding. He is most unlikely to be anywhere in the open. No one need expect him to climb in at bedroom windows. His only wish will be to avoid you, unless cornered. The Keeper hopes so to arrange things that he himself takes the position of risk. He asserts absolutely that if a man stands his ground even a charging gorilla will give way, but to turn tail is fatal. As he has brought Hanno up from a baby he is confident of being able to manage him. "We don't want him shot," he says. "Quite apart from his money value and rarity, eleven years of handling would be wasted, and Hanno is considered the finest specimen in captivity." Supposing he is not in the Park? our correspondent asked. "That would be another matter altogether. It would be really serious. I am afraid it would be out of my hands. But if he is not here, where is he? Nobody has reported anything. He must be here. He's clever and cunning, and not so conspicuous as you might think. It's not a shape that detaches itself from shadow and trees. His very bulk camouflages him. But we'll get him. Keep calm, keep away and leave it to us," was the Keeper's advice.

"Are you sorry you left London, Ping?"

"No. It sounds horrid. I wish Hanno had let out all the lions and snakes like I thought, so that it wasn't everybody after one."

"Those big-game hunters are to help to catch him alive, not to shoot him."

Ping looked at the little old lady who was no bigger than himself and soft like a bird.

"You can't imagine how strong he is," he said with his funny smile "My arms can't stretch as far as the width of his back, and his muscles roll about under his skin like logs in a mill race."

"I can see you know the river well. Would you like a boat today? It's going to be very hot. I am sorry that when I knew Tolly wasn't coming I lent the canoe to a friend for the holidays. But we can hire one for you."

However, Ping's interests this time were centred not on the river where he would have missed Ida's and Oskar's company, but on the Thicket. This was partly because he had overlooked its possibilities before, and partly because for the last few weeks his imagination was continually returning to forests.

He went out first thing after breakfast to explore the Thicket. This was not easy. It had originally been planted with oak and pine as a screen and background for the garden.

76

At some time it had been felled for firewood and had sprung up again, so that where one big trunk had been there were now five smaller ones. Trees too big for sawing had been left standing. Through the centuries the birds had added seeds of yew, cherry, dog rose, hawthorn, elder, ivy and hop, till it was as impenetrable a thicket as you could hope to find, with here and there in deeper shadow a patch of clear ground under the biggest trees. Wherever there was a space left by a fallen tree, the grass and wild carrots were waist high. Ping was slender and very easy in his movements. He slid round trunks and edged through chinks, and saw no sign anywhere of human intrusion. It was not like the beginning of the world—the Garden of Eden would surely have been more luscious, with pineapples and grapes—but perhaps like the end of the world when man has been and gone. The sun played with the polished and tender leaves, picking one out here and there, and leaving another as a mere twiddling shadow. It streaked each bright stalk with the shadow of its neighbours. It penetrated steadily down among the trunks to warm the tumbled bedding of the earth. The birds seemed more inquisitive than resentful of Ping's quiet presence. Certainly it was a Paradise for them where they themselves had planted seeds of all their favourite fruits; where the ivy climbed even the yew trees and doubled their summer dark and the winter shelter that they offered; where the ground was never raked and those birds who prefer to take cover there could have grass huts absolutely weather-proof. Ping felt that a thousand miles, a thousand years separated him from the International Relief Society's Intermediate Hostel. Then softly parting with his hands the bamboo through which he had been pressing, suddenly he saw the blue and brown water of the moat, and beyond it the kind walls of Green Knowe.

Mrs. Oldknow was standing on the farther bank cutting roses off a rambler that hung down out of the sky, where it had climbed up an elm tree. "Hullo, Ping," she called, "how right you make the bamboo look! What a pity I haven't a willow pattern bridge for you."

"It doesn't look deep. Can I wade over to you?"

"Don't be deceived. It is deep and treacherous. You'll have to go back the way you came. There's only that one bridge."

"May I make a hut in the Thicket?" he asked at lunch.

"You can do anything you like so long as you don't make holes in the bramble hedge or in any way make it easier for outsiders to get in. Or spoil the bamboo as seen from the garden side. Or make bonfires and burn it all down. Above all, no bonfires."

In exploring the wood Ping inevitably made faint tracks of broken twigs or brambles pushed to one side. He tried to keep to these, partly for ease, partly in order not to lose his way, and chiefly to disturb as little as possible the wildness that pleased him. He gave his landmarks names. There was Fallen Elm, there was Hazel Clump, there was Ivy Cavern where ivy grew so thickly over a dead tree that it hung down like a tent and one could go inside where even the tree was hollow. There was Big Bog and Little Bog and Wild Rose Barrier. Much more remained to be explored.

Ping chose a place well inside the wood at the edge of the bamboo, where a yew and an oak disputing the right of room and light between them kept a stretch of ground underneath clear of everything but ivy and dead leaves. Ping's plan was quite clear in his head. First he had to flatten out a circle in the middle of the bamboo. He began by trampling down a cane at the root. It slid down among the other polished canes quite

He sat down to enjoy it.

easily and laid its length on the ground. He then did one in the opposite direction and two at right angles so that he had marked out a cross for the measurement of his circle. After that, slowly and carefully he trampled down all the canes in a circular space, coaxing each one down so that it broke nothing outside his ring, even when its feathery head lay outside. His floor was thus a rather lumpy matting, with the bamboo thicket still standing upright round it. The next step was to loop a length of twine round the nearest standing canes in a ring, draw their necks together and fasten them tight, so that they made a conical cage with a high crest on top. This simple design took longer than one might think, because of the difficulty of moving among stems too close together to allow of a step, where soft but pointed leaves were always projecting at eye-level. However, when finished it was charming inside, quite roomy enough for a boy, while outside it was almost invisible, lost in the surrounding bamboo that stood un-damaged because Ping had worked from inside. He sat down to enjoy it. Through his entrance he could see the open ground under the two big trees. The earth smell was close and strong. The sun filtered through everything, making a pattern of shining ovals in the shadow like the rice grains in his mother's cups. Where such a sun fleck fell unnoticed on his arm or leg he would suddenly become aware of its burning. The sides of his hut were still open. It was a very pretty token of a hut, but tomorrow he must close in the walls. His in-conspicuous track went on past the doorway, and on the right he could see Ivy Cavern.

Now that he was not making any noise himself or shaking the bushes, he could listen to what went on in the wood. There is very little bird song in August, but families of young birds were playing together, chasing each other round and

80

round with high spirited twitterings. Under the big trees blackbirds were scratching for insects, turning up as much earth and dry leaves as a farmyard cock. Until he saw them doing it, Ping had been inclined to think there was a man raking somewhere. Pigeons too make noises that are really startling. Even a man would not make as much noise as that, unless very startled. Perhaps the pigeons had been startled. There was a surprisingly insistent buzz of insects throughout the whole wood, not loud but vibrating like the heat shimmer off the earth. He listened more carefully. Funnily enough the overall hum of insects by being so continuous seemed to emphasize the quietness. Every now and then came the sharp crack of a twig for which Ping was at a loss to account, and somewhere a wren was scolding. Bamboo branches were brushing against each other. Of course when a bird flies out a branch springs back, but sometimes no bird flew out. He felt sure there was a lot going on in this wood. That is the charm of woods, anyway. Things live and breathe quietly and out of sight. You can sense it, but you don't know what, or even if it isn't the wood itself, more alive than it seems. A moorhen startled him with its panic squawk, and he could hear it crossing the moat somewhere behind him, running on the surface and using its wings at the same time, till with a swish through the water it reached the garden side, where it clucked in agitation from under the reedy edge. There was a loud crackle of bamboo canes. The moorhen took off again and flapped shrieking farther upstream. When its clamour died down, Ping heard what he first thought was someone splashing their hands in the water. Or could it be a big dog drinking? A man then with a big dog? Mrs. Oldknow's poacher? Ping was indignant. This was his wood, in which he was happily imagining—what he was imagining. He certainly didn't want

F

poachers. He thought he would go and tell Mrs. Oldknow.

She had visitors for tea. They sat in the hidden garden in the shade of a tree, for it was still very hot. They were all grown up, but seemed intimate friends and there was much affection and laughter. Mrs. Oldknow said to Ping "You must please be my grandson", and he handed things round for her with a little air of ceremony, remembering as in a dream a similar feeling in his own distant Chinese home. He felt no need to speak but enjoyed the occasion from behind his barrier of deference. Mrs. Oldknow's face had an expression that he knew suddenly he was already very fond of. He stood behind her chair and from there took in the laughing ease that never, never comes into camps or hostels. Mrs. Oldknow turned to him.

"Ping, my dear, if you want to hear the six o'clock news, it's nearly time. Come back and tell us if there is anything special. He takes a personal interest in the escaped gorilla," she explained to the others. Ping made his bow and sped off.

"The gorilla Hanno may be in Hertfordshire or Bedfordshire. It is now certain that the missing gorilla is not in Regent's Park. It is possible he may be drowned in the canal, as gorillas do not swim. There have been no reports from outside of his having been seen. Only one clue has been received as to his possible whereabouts. A market-gardener from Huntingdonshire reports that he drove his covered van up to Covent Garden on the night of Tuesday last, the night that Hanno disappeared. He delivered his load of flowers, and met a friend whom he obliged by taking an emergency load to Victoria Station. In return for this he was given a crate of melons to take back as a present for his family. He started on his return journey about 2 a.m. It was quite dark, and as he was tired he decided to take a snooze in his cab. In order not to be disturbed by the main road night traffic he turned off and pulled up against the Park at Hanover Gate. He woke up with a feeling that the van had been jolted. He leant out, saw there was nobody about and thought no more of it. He drove on through Baldock along the A 14, stopping three or four times to try and improve his lights which were flickering badly. He also pulled up at a lay-by behind another van. It was half light, the most trying time for the eyes. He smoked a couple of cigarettes with the driver of the other truck, and then continued on his way. He does not remember exactly where each of his stops was. On arrival, going to the back of the van, he discovered the crate of melons broken open, and half of them eaten or spoiled. The quantity gone was enormous and the residue lying about showed that it had been eaten on the spot. He now suggests that the gorilla might have boarded his van during his first pause and left it during any of his subsequent ones. The police have been alerted along this route, and as soon as there is the slightest confirmation of a most unlikely theory, warning will be given in the areas concerned. In that case the Keeper and his expert assistants will move up with the Zoo van to the nearest point and will work in close co-operation with the police. The Keeper says that Hanno has always had a strong objection to trucks passing through the Zoo. But since he has got away, it must be considered as a possibility that he got in a standing van for food, and had an unexpected lift. He would probably jump off at the first stop if he could. In the wild state they do not travel far in a day, generally two or three miles, but if disturbed have been known to do twenty-five. If Hanno is really at large it continues of the utmost importance not to harry but merely to locate him. The police will warn each district where a search is going on."

Ping danced off with skips, whirls and songs of excitement till he came within sight of the party on the lawn, where he cut down his display of feeling to a flighty walk, and dropped down to sit on the grass by his hostess.

"Well, Ping? Have they found him?"

"No," he answered impassively. "Not yet." But Mrs. Oldknow was beginning to know his face. She knew now that behind his private little mask he was bursting with happiness.

"Go on, Ping. I'm sure there's more."

Yes, but he could hardly bring himself to say it.

"Where is route A 14?"

"It's the nearest main road, about two miles from here. Why do you want to know?"

"They think Hanno jumped out of a truck somewhere along it two nights ago."

"Good heavens!" everybody exclaimed. "This is local excitement. Who said the country was dull? Give it half a chance and there's a gorilla behind the hedge when you walk home from the bus."

"I live in a street. Nothing happens in a street."

"I've never seen a gorilla," said one. "I don't know the difference between that and a chimpanzee."

"Oh there's all the difference in the world," said another. "A chimp always strikes me as gone downhill, a really degenerate species. They sit mumbling and grinning and scratching each other, treacherous, neurotic and hysterical. A gorilla is a stupendous creature, very up and coming. He seems to belong to the dawn of his time, the origin, not the end; the elemental stuff packed with compressed vitality, from whom everything is still to come."

"That's Ping's idea," put in Mrs. Oldknow. "Ping calls him a genie in a bottle."

84

"Chimps are supposed to be Aryan cousins. Would you say the same thing about the African and white races—that the Africans are up and coming and the whites going, going, gone?"

"I almost think I would," said the only man present. "In our big cities there is nothing at all not made by ourselves except the air. We are our own context and live by ourselves picking each others' brains. There's no vital force. Electronic Man."

"Well, but the Africans are following us as quickly as they can. They want to be electronic too."

"Then perhaps in the end, if we don't exterminate the gorillas before we exterminate ourselves, the gorilla will have his chance. He's one of the really great ones of the earth, and he's not specialized, he's versatile. It's the versatile who survive."

Ping listened to all this half understanding, wholly interested, but noticing with surprise that the idea of the gorilla's possible nearness had passed out of their minds, whether because it was too improbable or not particularly out of the ordinary for them, he could not guess. They talked, they had theories, but they did not believe. Unless perhaps Mrs. Oldknow, whose hand was resting on his shoulder, had thoughts she did not say. From where they sat he could faintly hear the rustle of the bamboo beyond the water, and the soft unruffled cluck of the moorhen. The life of the wood was quiet and safe, forgotten and unguessed. For, he realized with a start, anybody rinsing his hands on the far side of the moat could be heard and seen from here, where they were all sitting. Ping had a fit of the dry grins, and was obliged to roll over with his face to the grass, in which position he could feel his heart knocking in his ribs. And suddenly he began to wish desperately that the visitors would go, *in case something went wrong*. He dared not formulate it more clearly even to himself, because when the imagination is playing its highest game it is important not to let it come out into the open, lest reason should say Nonsense and the tension be lost.

The visitors were reluctant to go. The evening was so quiet, so wrapped about and timeless, with the old house standing like a guardian between the two gardens, the inner and the outer.

"What is so strange about Green Knowe is that no one can feel strange there. Isn't that so, Ping? It's a real sanctuary. Nowadays everything is changing so quickly we all feel chased about and trapped. Three years ago you might have escaped to the most unexplored part of Africa, and by now you would have the Kariba Dam and a large town. And yet here, in the heart of industrial England, is this extraordinary place where you can draw an easy breath."

"Nine hundred years isn't so long," said Mrs. Oldknow. "It's only a breath. The sort you take when you are asleep."

"If your lungs were *this* big," said Ping stretching his arms to full width, "it would be a big one."

"Quite worth taking," said Mrs. Oldknow.

When the visitors had gone, waved away by Mrs. Oldknow and bowed away by Ping, he helped her to wash up. He took the man's place at the sink and enjoyed handling the fragile china. He enjoyed the whole feeling of a real private house and the way it had to be looked after, not for discipline but for pleasure.

"My dear Ping, you are as good as a Chinese houseman and they are supposed to be the best in the world."

Afterwards he helped her to spray the rose-bushes. They

watched the starlings fighting for room to roost in the over-crowded ivy on the elm trees.

"They haven't gone back to the bamboo. I wonder if there is a fox there. You must look, Ping. I do sometimes see a fox in the garden. In the early sun they are as red as fire and very beautiful."

"Do you tell the farmers?"

"No, of course not. I let anything live here that wants to."

"So would I," said Ping, and said nothing about the poacher.

When he awoke next morning, wreaths of mist hung low over the river bank. The willows breaking through it hung like trees adrift in the sky. The boat-house might have been perched on a precipice for all one could see. It reminded Ping —of what? He searched in his mind and found an old old memory of a picture like a roll of wallpaper hanging in a house where a little boy learned to eat with chop-sticks. The mist was changing while he watched. He would have liked to keep it for a little, but it thinned and lifted and was seen to grow out of the water on glassy stalks. The ground was revealed as he knew it, but after the mist had risen to a separate layer, and the sun hazily fumbled through it, the garden and the islands continued to steam like a horse's coat. In the wood, which he could not see from any of his windows, what double privacy, doubly penetrating morning scents, for a fox, or any other of Mrs. Oldknow's unseen guests.

"Good morning, Ping. This mist means another roasting hot day. The dew will be boiled off before the plants have time to drink it. Will you see if the paper has come before you sit down, please?"

The paper was full of an aeroplane accident, a bus strike,

and an attempt to swim the Channel. Nowhere in it was there the smallest reference to Hanno.

"That's the worst of the papers. They never tell you the end of any story. It just drops out and leaves you guessing. Perhaps he is drowned, or has eaten rhododendrons and quietly died somewhere where he will never be found."

"Is rhododendron poisonous?"

"Very."

"What else is?" Ping asked anxiously.

"Laburnum, laurel, yew—the leaves, not the berries—deadly nightshade, foxgloves. Those are the most common."

"Are there any in the wood that—that I might eat by mistake?"

"Only yew, I should think. And you won't be eating the leaves! The foxgloves are all finished by now. Rhododendrons don't grow here at all. There might be deadly nightshade." She brought out a book and showed him pictures of the plant and berries.

"Will you be in the Thicket today?"

"I want to thatch my hut."

"Huts", said Mrs. Oldknow, "should have some kind of stores, as I remember, for moments of hunger. How about a biscuit tin with oranges, bananas and biscuits?"

"Thank you," said Ping, twinkling and thinking things to himself.

"And as you haven't got a watch and I haven't got a loud voice, would you like a picnic basket for lunch? If you get tired of being alone you can always come back and eat it with me in the garden. I don't want to get rid of you, you know. You say what you would like."

"I just like being in a forest."

"I'm glad there's enough of it to be a forest for you."

88

The tin box was slippery....

She gave him the biscuit box and a basket with sandwiches, a pear, chocolate and a bottle of milk. "I shall be here all day. If it is as hot as I think it's going to be, I shall just sit in the shade and be happy. You'll find me there."

Ping set out with provisions under each arm. He crossed the moat by the drive-bridge and took a path that passed through the kitchen garden. It was quite a walk to the gate of the Thicket. The tin box was slippery and angular and wouldn't stay comfortably under his arm. The basket was too heavy to hook on the little finger that was all that could be spared from holding the tin, and Ping needed his right hand to make a way for himself among the saplings. He expected it to get even more difficult when he had passed Big Bog and Little Bog and struck into the heart of the wood. He found however that since yesterday somebody bigger and more careless than himself had been there and had made a noticeable way through. He was annoyed. When he had first seen the Thicket beyond the bog it had been trackless, and he himself had been most careful to keep it so. A wood with a track, he felt, was a public wood. He wanted one that was sacred. He would have slipped through the brambles and branches to one side so as not to make the passage clearer, but his box and basket were too hampering. He had to take the easiest way. It led to his half-finished hut, and continued beyond it. It was however no more than a track, and unless he was following it he could not see where it went next. With relief he put his provisions on the floor of his skeleton tent. It was very pretty, he was charmed with it. The myriad boat-shaped bamboo leaves moored in threes to their stems floated motionless in the air. The sun was not yet above the wood. It shone through it from behind, so that small leaves like hawthorn and yew looked black, but the floppy oak or ash and particularly the bracken lit up to the emerald green of lizards. The bramble arches were often a perfect curve as if done with compasses, and the leaves that hung from them were like American cloth —shiny on top but cottony and cool underneath. Everything was still fresh from the night's mist and breathed and lifted in the warm air. Opposite the hut was a clear space beneath the interlocking oak and yew, some way to the right was Ivy Cavern. Ping surveyed it all with deep satisfaction. His business now was to roof his conical hut so that it would give shelter against a tropical storm, which after all might happen. The easiest way would be to heap dead grass and leaves over the framework. This was primitive, but there was plenty of material round his doorstep where it was surely proper to make a clearing. He began to gather armfuls and lay them in sheaves round his hut, layer upon layer, beginning at the bottom. It was not as easy as all that. The grasses and tall weeds were withered and half lying down, but had not been cut. It was not like picking up scythings. Each armful had to be torn and dragged out of a still living tangle. The floor of the wood was knitted into a continuous fabric of which the strongest strands were hidden brambles. Ping heaved and panted and blew flies off his lips, and his walls slowly rose towards the peak. The clearance round his hut though it made it more conspicuous also made it look more convincing. He kept his gleaning methodically to a small circle in front of it. At the farthest point on this circumference as he bent to pull on the dry straw, his eye came opposite an opening between branches through which he could see the base of Ivy Cavern. He stiffened as still as a tree. Would not anyone say that that dark hairy knobbly piece of ivy root sticking out of the Cavern was a gorilla's foot? Thumb and all. Long strands of ivy hung down over the opening and swarms of flies danced in the sun in front of it. Also a spider on a thread hung busily just in front of Ping's eye, confusing the view. Ping moved his head, looking first with one eye then the other. The ivy root did not move, as of course it would not. He was much tempted to go and look at it near to, but if you are not sure which of two things is real, then it can be either for you. There is no point in deliberately spoiling your pleasure. He pulled up his last armful, jerking like a dog playing tug-of-war. And he completed his hut.

The sun was now overhead. Ping was very hot, and out of breath, and tired. He sat down, leaning against his soft wall, taking an orange that he meant to eat. The air was heavy. He took great breaths of it, thinking it would cool and revive him, but it held nothing in it but sleep. He yawned, and presently with his head on a pillow of hay and his apricot legs stretched out in the sun, he fell asleep. His uneaten orange rolled out of his hand and trickled in a half-circle out into the clearing. While he slept, the wood with no human eye to watch and interpret, carried on its private mysterious life.

Ping dreamed of centaurs—horse bowmen who pulled bows made of iron bars, who, when they reared, had six legs and two bodies like insects, which was altogether wrong and beneath the dignity of a man. It was troubling and he struggled with the wrongness of the dream, because the centaurs were wise and commanding and every child at some time wishes itself a man-horse. The centaurs talked like horses. They blew grunts down their noses. Grunts, thought Ping, waking up. There ought to be a better name for that sound. It was a grand, happy sound. It continued, somewhere quite near him.

Is this a dream within a dream? he wondered, opening his eyes and waiting for what was to come.

Ping could not have moved if he had wished to.

At the edge of his clearing, pushing through the bamboo was an enormous shaggy shoulder, thrust up on an arm as straight and strong as a hunter's foreleg, but infinitely more dangerous and versatile—an arm, not a leg, resting on purposeful knuckles and thumb. The head must have been looking backward, for it was a long second before it came into view, crested, heavy-browed, characteristically held in a position midway between animal and man, low between the shoulders but with the black lightning-eyed face lifted, the coiled nostrils not soft like a horse's but aristocratic blue-black and unyielding. Out of each side of his mouth stuck a piece of bamboo cane, looking like the porcupine quill some savages wear through their noses. He came out into the open, his right fist grasping a cluster of canes torn up by the roots. There he stood, at large, his untried power incalculable and arbitrary.

Ping could not have moved if he had wished to. He was paralysed with the impossibility of either belief or disbelief. In any case he was watching so passionately nothing could have made him move. The very fact that Hanno was as great as he remembered him, was a shock. He had in his single-minded innocence, no feeling of danger. Who could mistake him, Ping, for an enemy? He remembered the sparrows that went freely in and out of Hanno's cage in the Zoo. He was like that.

Hanno crossed the clearing to the side shaded by the double tree. He sat down at his ease, snapping and munching bamboo stalks and spitting out the fibre. His bearing was different from what it had been in his boring cage—more certain and lordly. There he had looked about him as if resentful of everybody and everything, except the Keeper and offerings of food ungratefully accepted. Where the lions looked through the crowd seeing nothing, Hanno had looked with undying dislike, picking out particular persons to dislike even more. Now he spread himself, looked while munching at the wide oak under which he sat, at the hot blue sky beyond it, and dug with hands like mattocks into the ground beside him to pull up wild carrot.

Ping looked at the foot sticking out towards him with the thumb curled in. He longed to see Ivy Cavern to know if that root was still there. Because if not, Hanno must have known from the sound of tearing grass that he was there—must even have been watching him. Then he saw with a start of surprise that there was a heap of chewed bamboo fibre *and orange peel* on the ground quite near him. From which he concluded that he had already been inspected and passed as of no account while he slept. They had in fact already been together an hour or two. The introduction was over and Ping was accepted. He was however far too sensible and modest to presume on this. He drew up his legs and sat quietly hugging his knees while his banging heart told him the size of his adventure. He rehearsed for the hundredth time all that the Keeper had told him. Carry on as if you were minding your own business and he'll come to you. That had worked without his even intending it. He wondered what else he might be permitted to do that would not annoy. Perhaps climb trees. That would seem normal and harmless. If he sat still too long, that might seem inquisitive.

Hanno meanwhile had finished chewing his bamboo and was looking round for something to add variety. He stretched out his arm and picked off a blackberry shoot which he ate with interest but without enthusiasm. He tried ivy, and his face showed clearly that it was bitter and coarse. Then he leant forward to pull up a clump of sorrel, and to steady himself his other hand went up to a branch of the yew tree.

The yew yielded to his weight and fanned him as he swung the bough down and up with apparent amusement and pleasure. Then he snapped a piece off. Ping was electrified by fear that Hanno was going to eat it. In a flash he had imagined the fatal stomach pains, the groans and cries of his beloved giant dying, and to prevent this he leaned backward through the door of his hut and pulled the basket towards him.

"Hanno! Hanno!" he called in his fluting voice, as he rolled a pear across the clearing.

Hanno dropped the yew and rose to collect the pear. He stood on all-fours to eat it—that is to say, one arm was a leg and the other was for eating with, twizzling the pear delicately in his fingers and finally holding it by the stalk to finish off the core. Ping could not get used to the way Hanno's arms were dual purpose, equally good for whatever he wanted. It gave him great advantages which Man had thrown away when he decided to become two-legged. When Hanno stood on all-fours it could never suggest as chimpanzees do the awkward business of crawling. It was rock-like and noble, as erect as anyone could need to be.

Ping had taken a sandwich for himself when he rolled the pear to Hanno. He was hungry and his hand had helped itself. Hanno while slobbering joyfully over his pear fixed him with his sharp sidelong eyes.

The pear was finished before the sandwich. Without warning, the thunderbolt fling that had so often been stopped by steel bars came straight at Ping. He flattened himself against his hut and watched it come, simply thinking, as if it was to be his last thought: This is what Hanno is.

But the charge, all that power and weight, was directed not at him but at the basket, which the scything arm that might have knocked Ping's head off, picked up as if he were playing

96

Rugby. He swerved away with the basket clasped to his bosom, then stopped to look back at Ping. His look might have meant: Come on, chase me, or equally well: I take what I want and no one shall contradict me. In any case it was theft, not murder, and in his relief Ping laughed in a trill rather like a bird. Hanno, sitting with the basket on his knee, replied with a wicked chuckle. The basket which he examined was an old-fashioned kind having a handle across the centre and a hinged lid on either side. He looked like a very important gentleman taking a picnic in a quiet spot, having shaken off even his secretary. Ping admired again his appearance of being superbly well dressed—black bearskin sleeves, silver-grey shirt and opossum trousers, worn with style and pride as if he were fully conscious that he was turned out to strike the fear of God into lesser beings. But now he was off duty, enjoying himself in privacy. He looked first in each side of the basket to see what had been provided, and made his choice. The sandwiches looked ridiculously dainty in his massive hands, but he ate them one by one, taking his time and savouring the different flavours—egg and lettuce, cream cheese and tomato, brown bread and honey, and he glanced at Ping as if to say: That's something I never had served to me in the Zoo. He brushed the breadcrumbs off his sleeves and waistcoat. From the other side of the basket he had already had the pear. There remained a packet of nut chocolate and a bottle of milk. As Ping watched him taking the wrapping and silver paper off the chocolate as precisely as he could have done it himself, he realized that his lunch had already gone and could have made no difference to a stomach that size. Twenty pounds a day, the Keeper had said. While Hanno's head was tipped back drinking the milk, Ping opened the biscuit tin and pushed it forward with his foot as far as he could reach into the clearing, because Hanno's charge, even if it only meant alacrity and not anger, was something he had not got used to. It came back to him how he had been almost pressed into the furry ribs and had smelled the musky bonfire smell. This time Hanno ambled forward, but still his movements were shatteringly authoritative. It was impossible to imagine any human being, however exalted or powerful, taking hold of a box with such finality. There was no snatching, no boasting, no defiance. Everything was his by absolute right.

There was more this time to keep him busy—apples, bananas, and a big packet of chocolate digestive biscuits. Ping thought that if he was ever going to dare to move, now was the time to do it. All the hours that he had spent roofing his hut, Hanno had been there and had not minded. So though he did not know what would be the *wrong* thing to do, it seemed that anything not concerning Hanno might be all right. And it was important Hanno should get used to him and not bother any more than if Ping were the local squirrel. He took his opportunity and slid round to the nearest climbable tree and went up it, mounting into the canopy of illuminated leaves and taking his choice in the varied and balanced superstructure of the branches. The bark was hand-warm to touch, the air warmer and clinging. From the top he could look out across the extent of the Thicket and see part of the pasture land beyond it bright in the sun, and beyond that again another copse. The sun was on the decline, the shadows lengthening, but in the open it was blisteringly hot. Wriggling round in the fork to face the other way, he could see over the waving tips of the bamboo the semicircle of the moat and the trees on the far side crowding about the house. He could not see, because of the leaves beneath him, where Hanno's tracks lay in the wood, but he could see with some alarm, the inroads already made in the bamboo. At that rate of destruction it must soon be noticeable from the garden. He snaked himself out along a branch of his tree from which he could watch Hanno in the clearing. He was extracting digestive biscuits from the packet, nibbling them at leisure, watching the orange sun now caught in a flaming tangle in the tops of the trees. The sunlight streaked him with bars of light, and streaked the rose and sepia tree-trunks behind him, speckled his violet-black face with twinkling lights and shadows, and so painted him into the picture that there seemed nothing strange in his being there. From time to time, hearing Ping moving in the branches, he looked up, almost, Ping thought, with approval. When the last crumb was eaten he patted his belly to congratulate himself on it. Ping too heaved a sigh of relief. At least he's full.

Hanno stretched, rolled over on to his back and with his hands behind his head and his legs crossed, lay swinging one foot, blinking at the sun and watching the birds settle in. Finally he rose and began to move round the clearing as if examining the position. He paused in front of Ping's hut, passed on a little way, and then standing up he seized a growing cane with each hand and began a construction the opposite of Ping's, weaving the canes loosely round each other to make a springy hollow. The work was accompanied by continuous grunting as if instructing an imaginary family to follow his example. Next he began to pad it and fill it up with grass. What a back he bent to his gleaning! Passing in and out of sun and shadow holding half stooks above his head, he cast them in his bed. As the sun fell he settled in. Ping saw his foot catch the orange light, then it was drawn in. Comfortable snorts closed the day. As quickly as possible Ping came down on the far side of his tree and slid away along the now familiar track while it was still just light enough to see. From time to time he listened, but all was quiet. Tonight would be full moon, and under it in the tangled wood lay his own particular Sleeping Beauty!

Back again in the garden, he didn't know whether to linger for joy or to race from excitement. He was coming back from an earthly paradise, and wherever and whatever that is, we may be sure it is not dull. He had stood up to the challenge, the gorilla rocket launched at him, and had gained the right of admission. Had Hanno recognized him? He did not know and it did not matter. Everything was wonderful to him now. The heron was flapping home across the islands to the heronry, the swans climbed up on to the river bank and there raised their pointed wings high like Seraphim before folding themselves into white curves for sleep. The river was a lake of glassy fire, because the sunset was still in the sky, but over the roof of Green Knowe pale green daylight still hung with the evening star there again, and the rapt flight of bats. So many free things! And the house itself a guardian of happiness and strange thoughts, a keeper of secrets, into which he was taking one too big for him.

It did not occur to him that his experience was marked on his face. As soon as Mrs. Oldknow saw him, she took him by the shoulders and looked with approval and said laughingly "I think you've been riding flying horses".

"Why, do you know about the Flying Horses?" He had nearly forgotten them. That was a year ago.

"Every child has flying horses," she said. "Besides, Ida told me."

Ping wished he could tell her what was bursting him. But it was not his secret, it was Hanno's.

"In the garden today," Mrs. Oldknow went on, as if she

could read his thoughts, "I saw the two magpies and their five children. 'Seven for the secret that never can be told.' I always wonder if it would crush you, or be just too lovely. The young magpies are fully fledged and they make a very handsome party. You must have been enjoying the Thicket, you stayed so long. You missed tea, and you even missed the news. But I listened for you."

"What did they say?" asked Ping courteously but with noticeably less than his former curiosity.

"No trace yet."

"Oh." Ping's face had no expression except perhaps a suggestion of a smile. His eyebrows slid up a trifle towards his temples.

"You must be hungry. It wasn't a very big picnic lunch."

Why, she wondered, did he laugh out at that? His face was habitually under control, but his laugh when it happened was as spontaneous as bird song. He of course was thinking how much smaller his lunch had been than she had any idea of. And he certainly was hungry! It almost hurt.

"I can see you've been playing gorillas. You've got straw in your hair and yew needles in your sandals and bramble hanging on your collar, and your shins are grazed. There's a real Livingstone look about you." She picked bits off him and dusted him down, but there was no condescension in it. Golden boys to her were a wonder and a delight. "I'll get you a good supper to make up for your tea."

2

It was cool inside the stone walls of Green Knowe. In the garden it was now dusk, a reluctant dusk that was keeping an appointment with the moon, if it could wait long enough.

Ping, clean and brushed, loitered alone while he waited for his supper. He looked round him at the room, to which he felt desperately attached—desperately because a refugee belongs nowhere. The walls seemed to have forgotten they were ever quarried out of their own place and carried away. They had settled down to being simply stone again, reared up here by some natural action, smoothed and welded by sheer age, so that even when one came in at night and shut the doors and drew the curtains, the wildness of the earth was not shut out. It was inside in its most magical form—the cave wall. In this particular cave the table was gaily laid on a red cloth lit up with candles, whose small active fiery tongues made the dusk outside doubly dark and green and troubling. Ping spoke a secret into the house.

"*There is a gorilla in the Thicket*," and he added softly "*asleep in a nest*." It had been said, and was received for ever into the silence. The stiff finger-nails of a rose branch tapped at the window pane, and young owls to-whooed just to make the birds afraid, however well they were hidden. The house, like a perfect confidante, gave no sign that one more secret had been given it. Ping felt relieved and went to see if he could help Mrs. Oldknow in the kitchen. They came back together bearing dishes. It was a good supper indeed. He ate ravenously, and finally after two helpings of everything, sat back and involuntarily patted his stomach. He remembered Hanno doing the same, and he looked at Mrs. Oldknow and laughed. She answered his look inquiringly, so he said:

"It's a lovely feeling to be full." She smiled, thinking to herself that Ida was out-of-date if she thought Ping ate nothing. When they had washed up, and Ping had hung up his white apron, she said "You never wrote to Ida. Won't she be wondering?"

"I think I'll try now, please."

Dear Ida [he wrote, in his deliberate and original writing].

It is different here. I am not really missing you and Oskar because of something else. I can't possibly *possibly* tell you, in case this letter gets lost. But if you listen to the News, you might guess. I should think you would. Only if you guess, don't tell anybody, because it's a friend of mine, very special.

Mrs. Oldknow is much nicer than Miss Bun. I wish you were here.

Love from

PING

Ping lay in his bed and could not sleep. For one thing it was far too hot. The attic was the one room in the house not built for extremes of temperature. The sun had blazed all day on the tiles till the air trapped between roof and floor was insufferable. Ping threw off pyjamas and bedclothes and lay gasping under a sheet. Three open windows seemed to make no difference. The moon was up and the garden underneath was as bright as a mirror. That alone was enough to make sleep seem wanton waste. He felt compelled to get up from time to time to hang out of the window and look at the bewitchment spread out below him, wide and far. Only the Thicket, that violent trouble in all his thoughts, was out of sight, as if he had dreamed it. He went over the day minute by minute. Sometimes he dozed off from sheer exhaustion, and then the foot sticking out of Ivy Cavern would wake him up as efficiently as an alarm clock. The anxiety of Hanno's possibly browsing on the yew leaves never left him. He remembered his own voice shouting Hanno! How loud had it been? Could Mrs. Oldknow have heard it if she had been in the garden by the moat? What if someone else had heard—someone looking for mushrooms in the fields beyond? Perhaps it had only been a little pip-squeak noise. Nobody knows what his own voice is like. And how was he to keep Hanno fed so that he would never experiment with yew and deadly nightshade? At least Ping had as yet seen none of the latter. If he did, ought he to pick all the berries and put them in his pockets, or might Hanno be watching and only make a rush for them, thinking perhaps they were special? The supply of food in the biscuit tin, that Mrs. Oldknow no doubt thought would last a week, was all gone and would not be renewed. Ping had no pocket money with which he might have bought enough of something cheap for one day. Hanno, even if he did not poison himself, would have to move soon. And where else could he be so private and so safe? These thoughts tormented him, underlined as they all were with the sharp love he felt for Hanno, for his rock-like beauty and the terror of his authority, which was yet so vulnerable that a small homeless Ping was his only safeguard. For Hanno had many aspects. If he was so dangerous that police, commandos and hand-picked crack shots had to be put on his track, he was also cruelly displaced and wanting only to live. And Ping did not love him less because mixed with his huge splendour was a certain childishness and simplicity. He was of the same age as Oskar, and had the allure of youth.

At last he thought of possible action. He did not like it at all, but what must be must. He got out of bed and dressed very quietly, because Mrs. Oldknow slept underneath. He crept downstairs through the moon-flooded house, more arched and stony and hollow and secret-holding in this light than ever before. He let himself out through the living-room garden door. He knew the other garden by moonlight from last year,

The moon shadow of a thief

but he was not now thinking of antlered men or magic hunting dances. Something that might have been coeval with those distant spectres had burst into the present and filled it to the exclusion of everything else. Ping was engaged in theft. He went to the tool shed, by day a tumbledown wooden shanty, by moonlight a thing of sharp-edged mystery. He fumbled in its shadows for what he needed—a trug and a chopper. He followed the milky sparkling gravel path to the kitchen garden where Boggin's savoys stood in silver-indigo rows. He chopped down one at the end of each row, so that unless they had been counted no one would notice any gone. He did the same to the broccoli and the lettuce, and the French beans, taking whole plants and throwing away the pea-sticks. The silence in the garden was absolute and dreadful. He brought a rake and carefully raked over the ground where he had been. The moon shadow of a thief robbing his hostess raked beside him. When he had finished he was shivering. The trug was so heavy he needed both hands to lift it and had to stagger along with it bumping against his knees. How full of everything disturbing the garden was, how empty of everything reassuring! He toiled along to the gate into the wood, glad to get under cover from the finger-pointing spot-lighting moon. But here there were other thoughts. He did not know how Hanno would welcome night intruders, and Hanno by moonlight camouflaged in the black and white of a wood was even more alarming than by day. Ping went in only far enough to be sure the trug was sufficiently hidden. Fortunately Hanno was accustomed to long unbroken sleep, and he was deep in the Thicket. Ping's guilt and worry were left behind with the trug. It *must* have weighed twenty pounds, he thought as he frolicked back through a garden now appearing delicious and confederate. When he got back into bed, its warmth was welcome and he was asleep in a minute.

He slept long, and came down to breakfast late, ashamed and apologetic. Mrs. Oldknow just looked up smiling, and said, "I don't know how you will like this morning's news, my dear. Look at this."

GORILLA FOOT AND KNUCKLE MARKS FOUND SIXTY
MILES FROM LONDON.

Youths herding cattle into a mown field bordering the main road near Roman Well noticed curious prints in the earth which had been churned up by tractors in the gateway. The cows had passed in first and the tracks were much obscured. Experts have examined them and say they could be gorilla marks left three days ago, when the soil was less bone-hard than it is now after the recent hot weather. This tends to confirm the van-driver's story which till now was considered too unlikely to be taken seriously. These tracks if genuine give a point of departure for a new search, but the district abounds in small woods, parks and coverts, in any of which the formidable creature may be hiding. Search parties will be out from today. The police will warn each district where the search is to take place. The public are urgently warned not to try to participate in these drives, and above all not to get gun-happy. Quite apart from the value of the animal, to wound a gorilla without killing him is to commit suicide. Damage done to crops and orchards will be compensated. Domestic animals are in no danger, but dogs should be kept rigorously under control during the emergency. Meanwhile this warning to residents living between Penny Soaky five miles on the north of the main road and Long Potto six miles on the south—keep your children out of the fields and woods. There is no danger at all in the town, or in closed cars, or in your own home however isolated. All mechanized field work can go on as usual. Hand-picking of crops is safe enough if there is no cover near. Open country is the best safeguard. It is field workers who are most likely to be able to give useful information. Any person seeing knuckle marks, footprints with thumbs or wantonly broken fruit trees should report to the police. There is also a very characteristic gorilla smell, rather like the smoke from a bonfire of mixed rubbish, which hangs about where the animal has lain, especially where he has slept. All precautions are of necessity being taken, but the possibility of a hoax must be borne in mind.

The colour drained from Ping's face as he looked up agonizingly at the old lady.

"We needn't panic," she said. "That was the day he escaped. He may be anywhere by now."

"I don't want him caught." Ping could hardly bring it out.

Mrs. Oldknow sighed in despair at the inescapability of facts. "There's nowhere for him to be. Even if he covered twenty-five miles a night he'd never find his Africa. He'd only find Birmingham."

"He can stay where he is."

"If they let him, perhaps. But he would have to come out to eat. Get on with your breakfast, Ping."

But Ping couldn't eat.

"Must I stay in all day?"

"I can't help thinking that would be exaggerated. We haven't had a police warning here. What could be safer than the river, if gorillas can't swim? I've been in the garden nearly all the time and there's certainly nothing there."

"Does the Thicket count as your garden?"

She laughed at the seriousness with which he took it.

"Well, you have been in it for the whole of the last two days. I think you would know if there was anything there. Unless he moved in last night."

"I was there all last night too," Ping improvised desperately.

"You were there last night! Heavens, my dear child! I thought you were safe in bed. Whatever were you doing there at night?"

"It was so hot I couldn't sleep. I thought of my hut in the moonlight and went there."

Mrs. Oldknow looked at him with her bright robin's eyes.

"I saw your fox in the early morning. He was as red as fire, like you said. And the sun came up red like a Victoria plum. I went right across the wood trying to see where the fox had gone. But I lost him. Then I came in and went to bed again upstairs." These quick lies were told unhappily but manfully for Hanno's sake. Those who help prisoners to escape must lie.

"That seems to clear the Thicket of suspicion for today, then. I can't believe we have a resident gorilla. It is too fantastic. That's right, Ping, eat your breakfast. It's late. I'll go and telephone my friend the Inspector at the Police Station and see what's going on."

The Inspector was snappy. "No, Madam. Yes, madam. There's no need for the entire public to get in a panic. We are answering calls here all the time. Is the gorilla near my orchard? Can I put the baby out in the pram? Would it be safe to take a picnic to Coltsfoot Hill? And so on. There's only one gorilla, Madam, if there's a gorilla at all. And nobody has the slightest idea where it is. Personally I think it is a cock-and-bull story. My advice is to carry on as usual. All that's happened so far is a couple of blurred marks that might be a boy's prank. If an animal like that had been around here alive and loose, somebody would have been bound to see him by now."

Mrs. Oldknow repeated this last sentence to Ping who was brightening visibly.

"Yes," he said, spreading marmalade dreamily on toast, "somebody would have seen him by now."

"Let us go down to the village and see how everyone is taking it. It's always fun to hear people talk. The shop's the meeting place. I would like you to carry the basket for me."

Ping of course was longing to get to the wood. He had to make sure Hanno was still there. Till he knew that, he could hardly draw breath. While Mrs. Oldknow was writing lists and changing her shoes he sprinted round through the already sticky heat of the garden to the gate and into the trees as far as where he had left the trug. His offering had been accepted. The trug was gone. He was back a little breathless by the front door when the old lady came out.

"Hotter and hotter," she said. "Will you paddle me up the river today? It would be a treat for me."

This was a courtesy and a duty, and in any other circumstances a pleasure, which Ping now felt as an impossible sacrifice to ask of him. He must, and yet he could not. Instead of finding the old lady's pace too slow for him—though it was a brisk little trot—he felt dragged along. They walked by the river, where the swans, revolving to be in readiness for crumbs, made fan patterns on the water. The sound of ripples, the thought, as vivid as a sensation, of the cool and immediate happiness of water receiving his body as he dived, only added to his misery. All his will was elsewhere. They reached the boathouse and he heard the dreadful words, "Can we have a punt for the day?" And then unimagined salvation. After reading the morning paper too many people with holiday children to entertain had had the same idea. There was no boat left.

"I am sorry for your sake, Ping. I am not entertaining you at all well. It is lucky for me that I have a visitor who seems able to amuse himself without company."

Ping smiled mysteriously. But perhaps, she thought, all oriental smiles are a little mysterious.

They went on together to the village shop, where everyone was talking gorilla. Ping listened astonished at the vagueness, the inaccuracy and the silliness of grown-ups. Someone was coming out as they went in.

"Good-bye. Mind you don't meet that monkey," came from inside.

"It isn't what you'd call a monkey," someone corrected. "It's bigger. It's a kind of chimp."

"I don't know why they make such a fuss. There used to be one in the Zoo that was so tame that you could have your photo taken with its arm round your neck. My dad did."

"They say this one can tear a man's head off as easy as screwing the top off a bottle."

"Then why doesn't somebody shoot it? That's what I say. Why don't they shoot it?"

"Here, Fred, you used to be in the Home Guard." Everybody laughed, turning to old Fred, who used two sticks for walking.

"That was Germans," he said, "not gorillas. Besides, we didn't really expect them." Laughter again. "And they weren't cannibals anyway."

"I always thought mnokeys lived on nuts."

"That's squirrels, love."

"And how would you like to meet this gorilla, young man?" someone said condescendingly to Ping. "You'd soon bring him down, eh?" He made the gesture of shooting up in the air. "Have your photo in the papers standing by the body, eh?" He winked and nudged his neighbours.

"Bless his little heart," said a fat woman with a wide beaming face, as Ping looked round offended and antagonized. "Space men is all they think of now. They don't know anything about gorillas, do you love?"

"Yes," he answered coldly and politely. "I do. I saw Hanno in the Zoo. He's a kind of a man."

"Oh! Oh!" hooted a woman. "They're the worst of the lot. I'm going home to bolt myself in. Ta-ta."

It was now Mrs. Oldknow's turn at the counter.

"You're very busy this morning, Sally."

"We are! Everybody wants to get done early. Most people seem to be going in their cars to drive round and round and see if they can watch the fun. It will be like a Meet. Personally I think it's all a leg-pull. I know one of those two boys that found the marks. They're just the sort to enjoy a good hoax. You could easily print it with a bulky reinforced glove."

On the way home again down the village street, where they hugged the wall for its narrow strip of shade and the heat over the tarmac vibrated like television, Mrs. Oldknow said, "You know, Ping, children are supposed to live in make-believe, but their play is always practising for real things, whereas grown-ups' make-believe is a horrid triviality. What they read in the papers is only one degree different from what they see on television. Whether it is true or not hardly matters. Since Hanno, as you say, is a kind of a man, even if not our kind, ought they really to be driving round and round hoping to see him shot? I think I am as shocked as you are."

Ping was grateful. His heart was very heavy, because Hanno was real. If he was shot, it would not be like a film or television, but he would be dead, and that would be real.

The east side of the Thicket could be seen as they walked back. Ping raked it with an apparently careless glance, but it looked as innocent as he did himself.

During their absence, a neighbour had called and left a basket of peaches, with a note saying "I thought you might like these. A few are slightly bruised and those should be eaten at once." Ping's face, bent over the basketful for the smell, reflected both the colour and the joy.

"Do you like peaches, Ping?"

He nodded.

"How many can you eat? One? Two?"

He continued in spite of himself to look covetously at the luscious fruit.

"Three," she laughed. She picked three gold and crimson beauties and held them out. "Where's our little lidded basket?"

"I know," said Ping, taking the peaches and running off. "I'll get it." He was gone.

"It will be in the wood, of course," she thought. "Oh, well, I'm not going to be the only person in the country to panic. Fear is a symptom of feebleness and old age. Ping hasn't got any. He's a splendid little boy."

At the gate into the Thicket Ping stopped to get his breath and collect his thoughts. "I'm supposed to be about my own business, as I was when I built the hut. My business is to find the basket and the trug. I only hope that Hanno doesn't think they belong to him now."

H   113

He had put the peaches carefully in his pockets and now went in singing softly to announce happy intentions. The ridiculous song that came to his lips was:

> O *where and* O *where has my little dog gone?*
> O *where and* O *where can he be?*

Its inappropriateness made him chuckle as he peered right and left for something he had described as a kind of a man, but might just as well have called an outraged jungle god. As he went farther in, there were signs of Hanno everywhere. Cabbage stalks tossed aside and bean stalks hanging over thorn bushes; broken branches where perhaps the trug had been dragged through. At last he arrived at his hut. In the clearing lay the trug and the basket, and the remains of the feast. Ping walked steadily to them, put the basket inside the trug, laid his three peaches in a row on the ground and began to walk off, trug in hand. It was startling when just behind him Hanno like a thirty stone black spider dropped out of the branches of the oak and seized a peach that had barely left his hand. Ping continued to walk at the same careless pace as far as the edge of the clearing, and here he sat down, elated but a little wobbly at the knees. Hanno ate the peaches one after the other, leisurely, surprised and gratified, guzzling and fixing Ping from time to time. His eyes were lost in the shadow of his heavy brow, but the white showed as they moved and the glitter of the pupils. When he had finished, he advanced with a sudden rush at Ping and stood over him, the executioner's arms in thick glossy bearskin rising at either side of Ping's hips, their elbows turned out for the readier exercise of their power. And Ping knew the width and rolling muscle of the back they supported. The black snout—what else could you call it in this proximity—was barely a foot from his face, but above it the eyes were those of a fierce young man. A bully, but what eyes! The close-up of Hanno's face was backed by arching saplings and thick layers of leaves plastered against the sky. A surge of jungle heat and smell came to Ping from the ground and from the hot table of Hanno's body.

"There's no more, Hanno—that's all." He showed his empty hands and rolled on to his back, which he had seen small dogs do to plead helplessness when attacked by big ones. In that position what he saw most clearly was the bare black human chest, so human it *must* be supposed to have human feeling.

"Am I to be murdered for a peach?" said Ping, laughing because he preferred it to crying. He drew up his legs for protection. Hanno snorted, gave him a push that wasn't too rough, and lolloped back to hunt for the three peach stones which he retrieved and re-sucked. Then he stood erect, sauntered across the clearing and sat down beside Ping. Anyone would have thought he was lonely. Ping reflected that escapers must be very lonely often; that they talk to cats and horses who can't talk back or give them away. Hanno was used to his Keeper, and to crowds of people, whom he hated but at least they were there to show off to. "Now there is only me. I'll be Hanno's cat," he thought with his spontaneous trill of mirth. He was answered with a pleasant sort of stable noise.

Hanno looked relaxed and confident, so easily in possession no one would have thought of him as fierce. His mouth had a gentle set, his expression was thoughtful, even sad. Looking at him now, sitting like a young chieftain, Ping ruled out of his mind the word "snout". No. It was a long jaw. What was he thinking about? The Keeper whom he had left? Or that other forest when he was a child? Did that come back with the queer feeling Ping had had when he saw those cups that he

"There's no more, Har

hadn't even known he remembered? The Keeper had said Hanno never forgot. Sometimes he opened his lips as if he was about to speak. If only he talked he would be a man. But it was just his being both man and animal that made him Hanno. They had not much to say to each other, but the wood ticked and fluttered and baked round them, and clouds climbing up toward the zenith blanketed the heat down on top of them.

Hanno yawned. The cavern of his mouth was vast and of a startlingly rosy pink—pinker than one ever supposes one's own to be, but then humans can never open wide enough to let the daylight in. His teeth were white and short, except the canines, and though he could certainly give a crunching bite, it was not his teeth one would fear him for, but for something much more manlike, something that lions for all their snarl and ferocity have not got. After his yawns Hanno rose upright, looked casually at Ping as an uncle might at a well-behaved nephew, and ambled away into the brushwood. He came out again to get an armful of extra bedding and then settled himself in a rather carelessly made bed for his midday siesta, crouching face down and wriggling himself under the straw like a crab settling into mud. Ping marvelled that he was like so many different things. In this curious position he was practically invisible among the tree trunks and sprawling grasses. He certainly could hide.

Ping picked up the baskets and the biscuit tin and moved circumspectly homeward, tidying up the stalks and litter as he went. He threw these on the compost heap as he went by it, put the incriminating trug back in the shed and rejoined Mrs. Oldknow in the kitchen.

"Well, Ping, anything to report in the Thicket? You were a long time."

"The Thicket's quite all right. I walked about in it. If anyone comes we can tell them they needn't look."

"Were the peaches good?"

"Yes, thank you. They made my mouth water."

They lunched indoors because of the great heat outside. The one o'clock news repeated what had been in the morning papers, adding that the likelihood of a hoax must be borne in mind. A police dog had been taken to the spot, but had failed to pick up a scent, which in any case must have been three days old. The weather forecast was of thunderstorms probably severe in the Midlands and East Anglia.

"It doesn't need the B.B.C. to tell me that. My eyes and skin have been telling me for at least two hours," the old lady commented. "And did you see the thunderclouds coming up before you came in? After a heat-wave such as we have been having, it's bound to come. I hope you enjoy storms, my dear, because I do immensely. This house is a splendid observatory for them, and I always feel if it hasn't been struck in nine hundred years there must be some reason why it escapes."

Ping said he was sure he would enjoy it. Downstairs it would be like watching out of a cave. He had seen a good storm last year from the attic window, and afterwards there had been a flood. "Ida and Oskar and I got carried away in it."

"I remember. I read about it in the paper. I was interested because of course it gave this address. You were rescued from a windmill. Of course! That must be why Ida drew a windmill on her envelope. Was it a special windmill?"

"Very," said Ping, his face softly moulded over a suppressed smile. "It had a window upstairs *filled up altogether* by the eye that was looking out of it."

Mrs. Oldknow appreciated this.

"And did you all see it?"

"Oh yes. We all saw everything."

"Then you must have been very good company."

"Oh yes, we were." Ping thoughtfully scraped the inside of a potato jacket, remembering. Then he looked up. "But you are, too."

"Thank you, Ping. Ida said she thought we should get on. Now I am going to eat a peach. Could you manage another or would you rather have something else?"

"I would like one, please," he said almost in a whisper, because he was ashamed to seem so greedy. But at last he tasted peach for himself and knew why Hanno guzzled and wanted more even after three.

They went into her private garden. Mrs. Oldknow asked him to put her chair in the shade.

"I'll put it this way," he said, "so that the sun won't be in your eyes." And he turned its back to the moat.

"Thank you, Ping. I expect I shall have a snooze. It's too hot for me."

That's two, he thought. He lay down himself with his face on the grass, his arms and legs happily spreadeagled. It was a heavenly rest to be somewhere where that variable and incalculable whirlwind of muscle was not. He could feel the short grass printing its pattern of stripes on his cheek. His fingers were in it, pulling up threads of clover and moss. Out of one eye he could see a daisy barring the world, the most vigorous and robust of growths. He blinked and was dropping off to sleep, and that would make three. How long would Hanno lie quiet and unseen? Just as Ping was dropping into unconsciousness—and that it is a drop is proved by the jolt of the pull up, he saw as if his mind were a blank screen and this a slide thrown on it, Hanno's eyes looking into his, piercing, haunting, commanding. What was he doing now? What if he broke cover or was heard? So great a creature must sometimes make a noise, a bark or a call. Mrs. Oldknow said orang-utans *sang*. It was too worrying. He glanced up at her. She was asleep, her humorous wrinkles relaxed and merely serene, her face cupped in her hand.

Ping slipped away.

He took a bottle of milk out of the refrigerator, and one or two oranges. It hurt that she would think him greedy and unmannerly, but every time that Hanno drank at the moat he risked being seen by her, though by no one else, unless she had visitors. In the part of the kitchen garden nearest the edge of the Thicket there was a bed of carrots and onions. He would take some of those for tomorrow. As he stopped to look, his heart stopped too. There were footprints all over the soil— thirteen-inch feet with thumbs, and knuckle marks too—such as would have been made if Hanno had come beyond the gate (in search of him?) circled, and gone back again. No roots were pulled up. In a fever he fetched the rake and obliterated all the marks, terrified of being seen. But then what if somebody had already seen a figure certainly not the gardener?

Hanno was waiting for him. The first notes of O where and O where were answered by grunts that said as clearly as grunts could, "Hurry up there. Where have you been?" as Hanno pulled the leaves aside and showed himself. A jerk of his head signed "Come on, we are too near the open". Ping followed. I'm not his cat. I'm promoted. I'm his little gorilla.

The milk bottle was in the way. Ping held it out and said Here! and stood the charge this time without fear. All the same, the way Hanno took things! The white bottle hardly showed in his fist. He took it with him to the clearing, where he removed the gilt paper with his nail and poured the milk into his projected underlip. The empty bottle he hurled into the air. It flew clear over the trees and bamboo and plopped into the moat. Ping had forgotten that some of his Zoo tricks would come with him. There he hurled all his rubbish out of the cage, but had never had the chance of bottles.

Hanno led him farther than he had yet been, for in spite of his reassurance to Mrs. Oldknow he had by no means covered the extent of the Thicket. They passed last night's bed, and the one of the night before. It was shocking how much the bamboo was broken. Ping could not resist his curiosity to try the bed. He had to take a good leap to get in, but it was fun, and springy. As he bounced, clouds of bonfire smell came out. But Hanno was coming back at his three-legged canter with one arm free for business, whether because his bed was private or because Ping was not following as he should, he did not know, but he scuttled to put as many trees as possible between them, and then followed obediently. Clearly little gorillas must expect to be cuffed. And what if, having adopted him into the tribe, Hanno wouldn't let him go again? That was a thought. They settled under a beech tree, on sweet crackly earth covered with half buried nuts. Hanno ate them with large composure and time to spare, as if they were hard-centre chocolates. Ping swarmed up the tree, which towered above him like a lettuce-green parasol, under which he was diminished to a swinging, clinging bumble-bee. Lying out on a branch, he grunted to make Hanno look up, then dropped the oranges beside him. From up in the tree, the outside world was not so cut off as it seemed down below. Cars could faintly be heard on the circumference of the silence, where secondary roads ran a mile or so away. There was surely more traffic than usual. In the distance he could just hear the far-carrying nasal tone of a loud-speaker van. Ping climbed to the very top, to inspect the land from there. The leaves were now beneath him, sloping away in glaciers of green, looking almost solid enough to slide down on. From here he could see the thunder-clouds building up their towers all round from the horizon, jostling sky-scrapers, some dark and some dazzling, that seemed trying to meet overhead, from where the choked sky sent down only a greenish light into the suffocating air. It was almost too hot to see properly. Ping's eyes felt dry and prickly as he searched the edge of the copse beyond the meadows, where he thought he saw movement. Yes, a man. Two men. They were walking slowly round the far wood, pointing and gesticulating. They met others and conferred with them. They slowly crossed the meadow towards Toseland Thicket. One carried a gun and the other was a policeman. They indicated the Thicket with a sweep that included the orchard, and the policeman pointed beyond that to where a belt of trees bordered the river. They seemed to be planning some future operation but not threatening anything at the moment.

As soon as they came within earshot, Ping called and waved like a boy who wants to be noticed. The men stopped, and one pointed up at Ping.

"Search this wood," he yelled, "I'm a gorilla. I'm dangerous."

"Kids!" said the man with the gun tolerantly.

"I'm a gorilla!"

Hanno at this had risen to his feet, and with an angry scowl hit the bole of the tree with his hand.

"Shut up, Charlie!" said Ping, lest the men should have heard. They shrugged and passed on, too official to wave.

Ping heard the policeman say, "That boy shouldn't be there." The other answered "Well, at least the gorilla can't be. We might almost leave the wood out."

Two men.

Underneath Hanno prowled round with his hair up and an air of savage responsibility. He followed the voices along on his side of the bramble hedge, economical of movement and making no sound, standing erect as he always did when his authority was in question. Sometimes Ping lost sight of him, and then it was difficult to find him again. Among trees he was tree-like when still, fluid as shadow when he moved. Ping could see the men all unconscious, walking away towards the river. They must have continued and completed their tour in that direction. They did not come back. Ping continued to keep watch till all the other men had gone off again towards the distant roads from which they had come. The clouds were now rocketing up in the dead centre of the sky, black and ready to burst. He was coming down from his tree when he really did see the fox. It stopped not far beneath him, sniffing the air, its scissor-sharp nose and ears testing the wood. Ping guessed it had had a near miss with the man carrying the gun. But Hanno was an unknown quantity to a fox. Who knows— he might have a sling and stone. The fox turned tail and went off in long bounds, its splendid brush nearly as big as its body, and disappeared into the densest bramble. Ping continued climbing down in the awkward, careful style of those who have no thumbs on their feet. Hanno had returned to the beech tree, looking up inquiringly to his scout. His black face was creased, his eyes darting, but his movements were menacing and controlled. "It's all right now," said Ping.

The Keeper had always talked to Hanno, so he must understand at least as much as a dog, and nobody knows how much more. He ambled off and could be heard drinking; could be heard perhaps by Mrs. Oldknow. She was not at all deaf, but luckily she didn't see very well, as Ping remembered to his comfort.

The idea came to him to try if he could draw Hanno away by rolling over and squealing as if he were being attacked. It worked. But when Hanno had looked right and left for an aggressor and found none, he gave Ping an impatient rap with the back of his hand which left him sitting holding his arm which he felt must be broken, and repenting of experiments. Not for long, however. It would have been funny if anyone else had seen it. Ida for instance. Also it was a matter for sky-high personal pride that he had such a protector.

He longed to stay and watch Hanno's nest-making again, but his bad manners to Mrs. Oldknow were very much on his mind. He had no idea how long he had been away. In extreme excitement it is difficult to keep an idea of time. Also he was haunted by the Keeper's story. If Hanno decided to keep him, they would both be in serious trouble. He slipped off with great cunning, going up this tree and that tree, making nests, trying them out with dissatisfaction, making another and so working round to his escape. Phew! What prickly heat!

Mrs. Oldknow was by the river, studying the clouds and fanning away the flies with a folded paper. She waved when she saw him coming.

"Oh Ping, you deserted me again. I slept too long and then found you gone. I don't blame you—it was dull for you. But I was beginning to worry, you were so long. It's much too hot for me to go searching for you. Sometimes Tolly's little dog Orlando disappears like that. I don't know where on earth he's gone and it makes me tired thinking of all the places he might be in."

"I didn't want to leave you." Ping was really unhappy about it, and perhaps for that reason she believed him. He has some sort of a secret, she thought. Something perhaps left over from last summer. A queer friend he visits—an ill child he takes peaches to? He's not greedy. She was an astute old lady and had confidence in Ping whenever she looked at him.

"You missed your tea again. Perhaps you don't have tea at the Hostel?"

"I took milk out of the refrigerator. And two oranges, without asking you. I'm sorry. It was rude."

"Strictly speaking, it was. But I expect it seemed sensible, and after all I was asleep. Who are these people coming up the drive?"

A car pulled up by the front door, from which two gentlemen and a policeman got out. The policeman rang the ding-dong at the front door.

"Run and tell them I'm coming, Ping dear."

Two of them were the men he had seen from his tree. Then he was high above them in a position of quite particular superiority because of what he knew and could see which they couldn't. Now the advantage was all on the other side. The policeman looked down on him, rocking from heel to toe with his hands clasped behind him. The man who had carried the gun wondered if this well-mannered slip could really be the publicity hunting child that had bounced in the tree. Ping saw that he was red faced with a lot of red hair on the back of his hands.

"Is it our young ape again?" he asked with a smile. Ping was grave.

"Mrs. Oldknow is just coming, please."

They turned to meet her. The policeman stepped forward.

"Good evening Madam. These gentlemen are Major Blair and Mr. Durrant who are investigating the rumour about the missing gorilla. They have both had experience in Africa and have volunteered to do this for us."

"Mrs. Oldknow, I believe," said Major Blair. "Forgive us for bothering you. We are planning tomorrow's search and have already examined Gibbs' Copse and the outer-boundary of Toseland Thicket, which I believe belongs to you. I must congratulate you on an almost impenetrable boundary, but there are one or two places where an entry would be possible if you didn't mind thorns, though there is no sign of anything having done so. You have I suppose a gate for your own use, which we would like to see. The constable here tells me the Thicket is cut off from the garden by the moat. Would you allow us to see the lie of the land on your side? You are, I am told, in the fortunate position of being on an island? Fortunate, I mean, from the point of view of safety."

"Certainly come round and look," she answered, leading the way into the hidden garden. "You will see the curve of the moat round behind that belt of trees. It runs into the river at each end. The moat is about ten feet of water over centuries of ooze."

"Can you cross from the garden?"

"No. The only bridge is the one in the drive, where you came in."

"Why!" they exclaimed as they came round the corner of the house. "This is entirely hidden from everywhere! No one could know you had such a place. What trees! It's a wild paradise. It would be a pity indeed to have such a garden smashed up by a great beast."

"Or a hunt after him, if I may say so, Major Blair. There's no gorilla here. I spend all my time in the garden, I know every inch. I know all the birds and should notice at once if they were disturbed."

As she spoke she remembered the starlings. But that of course was Ping's doing. "As for the Thicket across there,

Ping has lived and slept in it for three days, and all he reports is a fox."

"I've got a hut there," Ping burst in, "and paths. I play gorillas and make gorilla nests and break branches, and . . . fake knuckle marks with the gardener's gloves. If you find anything there it's all me." He felt that they took no notice of him, and raged inwardly.

"Have you missed anything from the kitchen garden, Mrs. Oldknow? The gorilla must have eaten, if he is here."

"I don't know. The gardener is away. He always brings in the vegetables. We can go and look. It's on the way to the Thicket."

The policeman and Mr. Durrant went with her, Ping of course hanging on anxiously. Major Blair with the gun stayed behind to look at the inner garden and the moat. Nobody noticed in the kitchen garden that there was room for one more plant at each end of each row of vegetables. All was nicely raked and orderly, except that Ping now noticed with horror that he had left the rake propped up against the railings.

"Gorillas eat enormously," said Mr. Durrant, "and spoil more than they take. Your gardener apparently raked here just before he went away, and there's not a mark on it." Major Blair now rejoined them thoughtfully. They were standing near the gate into the Thicket.

"If I hadn't your word for it that the boy's been larking round in there the whole time, and of course we saw him there ourselves, I should say it's about the most likely place for a gorilla we've seen. In fact there is everything he could want —privacy, cover, water and enough bamboo to live on for quite a time. And we haven't seen that anywhere else. It would explain his not breaking out for food, which, if he is

128

really alive, is the big mystery. I shall have to make a report on this. We certainly won't need to disturb you again in your garden. If we decide to comb the Thicket you'll be given warning tonight. And of course we'll get your permission before we cut anything down."

"Cut anything down!" Mrs. Oldknow went strawberry-red with anger. "I won't have anything cut down. It's a bird sanctuary. Nothing is to be disturbed. You haven't had my permission even to go in."

The policeman cleared his throat and grew a little larger.

"It's in the public interest, Madam, and for your own safety."

"Why should anything be cut down to look for a mythical gorilla? There's nothing in that wood but birds and Ping."

Major Blair, with his gun under his arm, was more tactful.

"We entirely appreciate your point. There is always the possibility—the probability—of no gorilla. What we are really trying to do is to allay public fears. We have to follow up this gorilla legend to disprove it. We have seen so far nothing at all to support it, except yesterday's famous prints at Roman Well."

As he spoke, he paused, his eye on the rake. He bent down to pick off something sticking in its teeth, which he examined. Ping's eyes had followed his movement and seen, before the fingers reached it, a spat out bit of chewed bamboo cane. Major Blair passed his find to Mr. Durrant, who said "Could be". They turned on Ping a very cold and questioning stare, but spoke to Mrs. Oldknow.

"Your excellent gardener leaves his tools out." Then with noticeably stiffer authority Major Blair pronounced:

"I don't want in any way to alarm you unnecessarily, but you will understand, Mrs. Oldknow, that if the gorilla is in the Thicket, where there is no other entrance but this gate, the Keeper going in to try to coax him out would have a bottle neck behind him where we could give him no protection, and the van would be at some distance, unless we drove it over your kitchen garden. The sensible thing to do, in such circumstances, would be to bring the van into the field at the back and cut a wide opening in your bramble hedge opposite it. You would hardly wish the Keeper to risk his life in a bungled attempt. We are trying to protect the public, the Keeper, and the animal. Meanwhile I advise you to keep in your island garden, and above all, keep that boy with you till we give you the all clear. Otherwise if anything happened you might be blamed for negligence."

During this lecture, Mrs. Oldknow was leaning familiarly on her own Thicket gate, disturbed by nothing but official impertinence. In the trees behind her a storm-cock was singing brazen notes of defiance at the clouds which were boiling up. Ping had stepped into the wood, but was ordered out. The policeman stood his ground facing the gate rather as one might stand on the main line when the express was due.

"With your permission, we will seal up this opening for the night. Would you bring that net out of the car, Durrant?" While his two companions went on this errand, Major Blair continued talking in an attempt to lessen the old lady's obvious hostility.

"We haven't sent for the Keeper before—he can't be spared for wild-goose chases. But it looks as though the animal could have been here, if he's not now. Nothing can be done tonight. Dusk is the time above all to avoid. They get suspicious and aggressive when choosing a sleeping place. We can have the Keeper and the Zoo van here by tomorrow morning. He is confident he can coax the gorilla back into the van, but of course we shall cover him in case anything goes wrong. He is a man of the most extraordinary cool courage. For after all, liberty, and still more pursuit, may have changed the animal's temper. However, they want him back alive."

The other two came back carrying a rope net such as is tied over loose loads on trucks. They festooned it across the opening with as many folds as possible.

"Don't pull it tight, or he could break it, or climb over it. It's to discourage by entanglement. We can't hope to keep him in by force. It may just prevent his strolling out to look at the weather and pick up a few carrots. We shall be here early tomorrow. You can't do better than stay in bed till it's all over. You will be kept informed. Constable, I suggest you drive round with the loudspeaker van and warn people that the gorilla may be in the vicinity. Don't say where or when. The last thing we want is onlookers."

"Perhaps we had better call personally at outlying or isolated farms?"

"We'll talk to the Inspector about that. He must give us more men to keep people off." They departed raising their hats in a way that neither lessened Mrs. Oldknow's fury nor Ping's fear.

"What insolence!" she said, her eyes darting like Hanno's. She was not used to being overruled on her own territory. "With my permission indeed! It was neither asked for nor given. I have their permission to stay in my own 'island garden'. Condescending asses! I thank them for nothing. Throwing their weight about like that. I can grow bamboo if I want, I suppose, without their permission. If it's paradise for me probably it is for a gorilla too. I can't help that. Cutting down my hedge! It will take years to fill up again and all the boys will be in after eggs." She tutted and clucked and was all fluffed up. She took Ping's arm and they walked back to the river where they had been before this unwelcome interruption.

"Pooh!" she said at last, calming down after watching several launches peacefully chugging along the tepid stream. "There's nothing at all in the Thicket. I've never heard such nonsense, but I suppose they have to do their stuff. 'My excellent gardener' indeed! What has it to do with them what Boggis does or doesn't do? What was it they picked up, Ping? I couldn't see."

"A bit of stick."

"They seemed to think it was very suspicious. I must say that if you and a gorilla have been playing Box and Cox together in the Thicket all this time it's an awesome thought."

"There are all kinds of thoughts," he answered. "And if he's there he doesn't seem to mind me."

"Who *could* mind you, Ping. But you must not go any more till they have searched. 'That boy' they called you, as if you were a criminal."

"I cheeked them."

"I am afraid I did too. But I was hot enough before they made me so angry. Those people on the river are going to get wet. Look at the sky! The storm-cock's never wrong."

The western sky was covered in a mass of troubled cloud of a sooty texture unnatural by daylight. Though the sun was behind it there was no gold-laced edge. It looked more like a flying haystack that was coming to pieces. To the east, dirty lemon-coloured cumuli were toppled sideways in what looked like a bubbling sea of lava. The air weighed on the lungs and stuck sudden needles into the nerves of the face.

"It's coming," said Mrs. Oldknow pointing to the west again. In the core of the advancing blackness, a green eruption was spreading round a hollowness, a funnel such as one sees at the centre of eddies, but big enough for the mouth of Hades. Out of it came a roaring express of wind. The trees in the distance suddenly had their umbrellas turned inside out and waved in tatters, the river was pressed down by a force that could be seen approaching. The boats swung in it and voices cried "Look out! It's coming," as SMACK came the full force of the wind, causing Ping to stagger and Mrs. Oldknow to cling to the gate post, her cobwebby white hair blown free from all its pins. There followed a cracking apart of the sky, lightning and thunder in one, and the rain came down as from a sky-syphon.

"Run, Ping—shut the windows!"

They ran, so buffeted and tossed that Ping might have been a detached willow leaf and the old lady a dress on the line. They were soaked before they reached the house. Laughing to be under shelter, they watched the people on the river enduring with screwed up shoulders and twisted faces their sudden and violent drenching as they made for the Boathouse. Ping dashed from room to room closing the windows. He and the old lady had forgotten their disturbing visitors in the excitement of the storm.

The rain intensified till it was almost unbroken water. It hissed, it roared, and Ping could no more see out of the window than if a hose had been playing on it. The lightning launched its sizzling missiles into the helpless earth while the thunder sounded like broken sky whose crashes and avalanches could be heard rumbling away in unimaginable distance.

Ping watched out of the leeward window in his attic. Darkness had come with the storm, but the lightning when it came was so bright it forced him to see more clearly and minutely than one usually can. Its passage across the sky from side to side was so rapid that all shadow was lost, the world appeared in an apocryphal light. It showed for a split second the whole expanse of the river and islands he knew so well. This was seen and lost, waited for, seen again and lost again. Sometimes he felt the seeing and losing were simultaneous, as if reality was intermittent or even not more real than unreal. When he focused in the dark on where he knew the garden was, and waited, the next minute showed him a brilliant colour close-up. The long leaves of the cherry trees were sloping gutters pouring water, streams were forming in the paths and running swiftly to make pools in hollows. Each flash gave a picture, illustrations from some book of high magic. The willows were white and demented. The bamboos lolled and swayed with the leaves plastered down to their stalks. As the streams and pools grew, the reflection of the lightning doubled its brightness. During such a display the thunder ceased to appal. It was the right and proper accompaniment, till one detonation was so close overhead that it did occur to Ping it would be nice to watch in company. Fumbling his way down—for he found the lights had fused—he paused to see the Norman hall appear sudden and exact, its leaning walls, its cracked arches and its cavernous shape. It was there and it was gone, more ephemeral than his memories of old temples. But the walls themselves were under his palms. Fascinated, he asked himself what he might see by lightning next. The outskirts of the hidden garden could be seen from this room. He opened the door leading on to a balcony. The cloudburst had nearly emptied itself, and the wind had dropped, but the electrical storm continued. Yew trees sodden and heavily scented almost brushed the walls. They drooped dark but silver-sparkled down to him. They

closed in the view. Over them was the flickering sky, beyond them the moat and beyond that the Thicket, unseen. What would the lightning have shown there among the crowded upright coppice stems or the rough angular arms of oak? In a shadowless wood, there is no camouflage.

Mrs. Oldknow was in her bedroom which was next door.

"We're in the dark", she called out, "since that last crack. Did it frighten you? This is a fine storm indeed. It is easing off now, but there is more to come. We must light candles and have our supper in the interval. Ha! That was a good flash. Ho! Crash!! Why does one enjoy it so much? Still, we must eat. You lay the table, Ping. Shall we draw the curtains, or shall we watch it? Let's draw the curtains and concentrate on our food."

They sat down together with the candles and the red cloth in the special seclusion and security of Green Knowe's walls. Instant news of the storm going on up above was relayed down the big open chimney. The thunder came down well, but the lightning diminished to a grey flicker over the soot.

Ping loved the meals he had with Mrs. Oldknow. There was just enough ceremony to make each occasion feel like a special one. It was not a discipline that cramped but a ceremony that one could play with and expand and even laugh at. It made him feel really at home. (He did it beautifully, *she* thought.) He cleared away the soup and put the risotto on the table.

"Has it been a real Congo storm?" he asked.

"Quite a good imitation. But I don't suppose it will last as long."

"I hope there will be a really bad flood so that we shall be cut off."

"Do you want to be cut off?"

"Wouldn't it be nice if the roads were flooded and no one could get here?"

"I see what you mean. But I think those tiresome men with their guns would be sure to have salmon-waders too. Anyway, my dear, we must want Hanno to be caught and taken back to the Zoo, because he can't live at large."

"I wouldn't mind if he wasn't quite alone. He's too alone. It is solitary confinement. Supposing he went white like an old man and was still sitting there."

"He has a very eloquent champion."

"Do you think he will enjoy the storm, if he is in the Thicket? Perhaps he will sleep in my hut."

"Do you really think he could *possibly* be there after all?"

"Just *possibly*. Wouldn't it be queer if he was."

"You make my blood run hot and cold."

"Why would it be so awful? He's almost a man."

While they were talking, the storm broke out again as bad as before, much like a man who tries to keep his temper down till quite suddenly it gets the better of him. It was bedtime for Ping, but he and the old lady sat for a long time in his room watching out of the window until they were too tired. She offered to make up a bed for him in her room, but he said he was not frightened, so she saw him into bed. As he took off his shirt a green and purple bruise was exposed that coloured all his upper arm. He looked at it with tender pride. That was Hanno's playful rap!

"Dear boy! What have you done to yourself?"

"It's nothing. It's just a knock. It hardly hurts now. But isn't it a beauty!"

"I believe a bruise is as good as a medal to a boy. You look really proud of it. Good night. Sleep late if you don't sleep

137

well. Remember we have to stay where we are tomorrow and you must *not* leave the garden. No slipping out tonight to see what gorillas look like by lightning," she said teasingly, holding his hand. "I wouldn't be surprised at anything you did, but don't! By breakfast time they will have found there's no gorilla there, and then you can do as you like again."

Ping clutched her hand to keep her, to tell her. But he only said "Good night". She put her hand on his forehead and looked into his face. It was as tough as it was fine and as candid as it was inscrutable.

"I wonder what you've got in your head," she said affectionately.

He did not however go to sleep. The lightning kept his room quivering in front of his eyes. It was almost never dark. The thunder was like cathedral roofs coming down, and even though his own bedroom roof stayed intact, he had to keep opening his eyes. But his real anxieties were quite different and far more real. Tomorrow at sunrise Hanno was to be rounded up, and he could do nothing about it. Even if he wriggled in under the rope net, how should he tell him, and even if Hanno understood, where could he go? This time his footprints would sink into the wet ground and be as easy to follow as a paper chase. Suppose Ping could concoct a plan for hiding him, Hanno was not one to take advice. He, not Ping, was the leader, and all too likely to go into battle.

Lying awake in the lightning-jigged, thunder-rattled night with the rain still pouring, Hanno's image came as clearly as if he could see him. This storm was real forest stuff and gave him back an illusion of his kingdom. Sometimes he lifted his blue-black face to receive the rain on it, streaming over his furrowed cheeks and into his mouth. He watched the lightning, which threw no shadow, turn the Thicket into an emerald-green vista of crowded boles and floppy dripping leaves. He looked for a dry place to make his bed, and every displacement of a branch precipitated the shower on his head and shoulders. The wet soft ground was lovely under his feet. The moss squelched and rose again. He felt the storm as a protection. As long as it lasted he would not be disturbed. It was home. He looked for his only dependant, who had strayed, and grunted to call him back.

Ping shot up in bed as if he had actually heard it, and clasped his head in despair. The thought of tomorrow was unbearable. He tried to think of it differently. Perhaps it was not so bad. Nobody seemed to think so except himself. Perhaps even Hanno knew that he could not stay where he was for ever. Perhaps it was just a wonderful unexpected holiday, like Ping's own, and must come to an end. There was that cage waiting—that railed-in empty square of concrete and nothingness—Ping's heart tightened till he could not breathe. Which would be worst, that Hanno should be shot, or that he should go back to it? Hanno himself would have to choose. Would he, for the sake of the Keeper, from whom he had never before been parted, of his own accord go back? Ping felt convinced it would not be for food and "security". It might be for his one real friend. For what was he, Ping, but a pretence young gorilla if Hanno was playing forests? He did not mind that he was nothing. He minded acutely that he could do nothing. What was going to happen, would happen, tomorrow.

He found he had been to sleep, and the storm was over. It was nearly light, and the thrush who always perched just above his window was singing the day in. The rain was over, the garden sodden and scented, the river full and rapid. The eastern dormer window showed a corner of the field on the edge of the Thicket, and there stood a van. Another stood on the bridge in the drive. Sounds of brushwood being chopped and pulled came to him in the stillness of the morning. There was the Major with his gun going through the kitchen garden. It was the day of doom. Ping dressed and went down. He let himself out through the living room door into the inner garden, walking like an automaton towards the moat.

It was a cruelly perfect morning, rich and steamy and scented, yet with some of the enchantment of night still clinging to it. It should have been a heaven for Hanno. He should have lingered curled in his bed, savouring the drip and rustle and privacy of his awakening. But there were voices, low-pitched and conspiratorial, but carrying, on all sides of the Thicket. Only the moat, deep and treacherous, lay unguarded. Ping walked desperately in the winding paths along the garden edge of the water, unable to keep away, unable to do anything there. All was silence in the trees. Then he heard the Keeper's voice calling Hanno, cajolingly as he made his way along the tracks. Ping's attention was so fixed on the Thicket that he bumped into an obstruction before he had become aware of it. In the gale of the night before, a small elm that had long leaned too far out over the moat, had let go of the bank with its roots and now lay across the water from side to side, its neck caught in the fork of a tree opposite, just high enough to prevent its flattening the bamboo at that point. From the other side its fresh wet leaves would look like part of the elm that propped it up. It was a perfect bridge, and no one knew it was there. Hanno, if he would, could cross it. He could hide in the garden. The Keeper's voice had stopped. Was it just that he had found one of the nests? Or had he found Hanno dead from eating yew? Ping climbed on the

... simply walking over him.

fallen tree and straddling it began to inch his way up its slope to the farther side. He heard with relief, the coaxing and calling begin again. Signs of Hanno must be all round him now, but where was the great runaway himself? Where was the giant black face with its disconcerting changeable eyes? Where the arms like branches of oak?

"Hanno, Hanno, you bad lad, come and see what I've got for you here. I've got something for you." If the Keeper could not see Hanno, it was certain he could see the Keeper. Ping reached the elm in which his pole of a bridge was jammed. He lay flat, hugging the tree and looking out through the double density of the leaves. His nostrils gave him the first hint. There was another arm looped round the same tree, and Hanno's face was almost cheek by jowl, looking the same way. It was a troubled, puckered face with wide nostrils, sharp but without ferocity. He held it lifted up which always gave it a peculiar nobility, and swung it from side to side as if weighing hard things.

"Come on, old boy. What are you hiding for? Aren't you hungry? Come on, I know you're there." The voice was gradually coming nearer. "Ah!" Perhaps he had found the second nest. But Hanno had decided. Abruptly he signed to Ping to get back where he came from. Ping began to slide down as quickly as he could. Hanno swung effortlessly up on to the bridge and overtook him midway, simply walking over him with the advantage of his four thumbs. He paused a second on the garden bank, looking back with the bright hard eyes of someone who decides to leave what he has most loved, and with a last brusque movement to Ping to follow him, disappeared into the bushes. The Keeper's voice passed the spot where they had been and went on beyond.

Ping looked around to calculate how much chance there

was now of concealment. There was plenty of cover, but far too much of it was yew and there was little bamboo. There was nothing safe for him to eat but beech nuts, and the beech tree was right in front of the windows. He ran into the house and skirmished round the kitchen for anything he thought would not immediately be missed. A bag of sultanas, a packet of biscuits, some tomatoes, a banana, a peach, a stale tea cake, and oh joy, a tin of condensed milk. He mixed this in an enamel jug and carried it out, together with all the eatables in a basket. He found Hanno sitting looking very miserable at the foot of a yew tree, his arms folded along a low hanging branch. It was always his variety of expression and character that caught Ping out. Now with his face resting in the crook of his arm, his features looked positively soft and his eyes melancholy. He looked suddenly so young. He accepted the jug of milk, cleared out the delicious sticky residue with his fingers, and handed back the jug. But he was in no mood for eating. The Keeper could still be faintly heard at the far side of the Thicket, and other noises too, speaking with less constraint. Their tones could be heard but not their words. They were evidently nonplussed. Ping emptied the basket under the bushes, to help to keep Hanno busy out of sight. He went and filled it with beech nuts and brought those back and added them to the store. Hanno still sat with his cheek resting on his arm, thinking unknown thoughts. Ping sat there awhile too, just to be company. But when you are improvising from one moment to the next, to stave off a crisis that is bound to catch up with you, it is hard to sit still. The great difficulty before him now was, how to keep Mrs. Oldknow away from the inner garden. The church clock struck seven. She would be getting up soon. He would take her breakfast to her, and make plans to keep her there.

He was too late. She was already up.

"How could anybody sleep—cars driving in and out as if it was a public car park. And look at all the people along the river path, climbing on my old wall and doing their best to push it over. Anyone would think it was a bull-fight. It's a wonder the B.B.C. aren't here. They probably are somewhere around, otherwise I don't know how all these people would have got to know. It's all very well saying I shall be compensated for damage. There is never any compensation for what the nameless general public does. I'm going to see if I can find a policeman to move them on." As she spoke the police constable and Major Blair arrived at the front door.

"Good morning, Madam. You will be anxious to know what is going on. The Thicket has been searched, and has revealed plenty of evidence that the gorilla has been there. But unfortunately he has got away, probably before last night when the net was put up, as there is no sign of his having broken through anywhere. Three nests have been found, which would suggest three nights, but your boy could have made some, as he says he did. One was in fact in the hut he built." Ping smiled, which made Major Blair look at him with hostility. "It is a pity he has been such an unreliable witness. For instance, the Keeper found a couple of cabbage stalks, which might mean that the gorilla helped himself from the kitchen garden. But if so, the beds had been raked afterwards, as we know they were because of the chewed cane raked up there. Now by whom were they raked?"

"Did you rake the beds, Ping?"

How he hated lying to Mrs. Oldknow! He stuck for words, but when the Major joined in—"Now young man, answer that question straight. Did you or didn't you?" Ping said quietly "Yes I did. I chased a butterfly all over the beds, and afterwards I raked it tidy."

"Had you seen any marks?"

"I was looking at the butterfly, not at the ground."

"How many nests did you make?"

"All but one. I found that. I thought a poacher had slept there. It smelled poacherish."

"And you never saw anything suspicious?"

"There was nothing to be suspicious of."

"Yet the gorilla was there, at least the first night."

"If you say so, Sir. But I didn't see anything. (That was true, at least for the first night). I found the nest later."

"You see, Mrs. Oldknow, it is extremely unsatisfactory. The gorilla was there, and but for the boy we should know exactly when he got away."

"You can't blame the boy", she answered, "for being perfectly innocently in a wood in which he didn't know there was a gorilla."

"Agreed. What troubles me is that though I distrust all his evidence, if he had seen a gorilla he would have cleared out of the way pretty quick. And why didn't he report the first nest? In any case, when found by us they were all cold. The one in the boy's hut smelled of gorilla. It's hard to tell how long the smell might hang on in an enclosed space. When did you build the hut?"

"The first day, but I didn't roof it till the second."

"He slept in it himself that night," said Mrs. Oldknow.

"Then that only leaves last night. But of course the gorilla may not have spent the night there. It might have been his midday snooze. We must now ask your permission to use the telephone to send for a police dog, though after that storm there is likely to be little scent. Another reason why we think he got away before last night is that there are no tracks outside the Thicket and the ground is now very soft."

"There will be plenty of men's footmarks I am sure," said the old lady peevishly, leading the way to the telephone.

"I know, Mrs. Oldknow, how very unwelcome and distressing this must be to you. But you must count it a miracle that the boy has escaped without harm. He should never have been there after warning was given on the air."

"You forget the gorilla was there two days before the warning was given. Hanno seems to have been and gone without doing any harm of any kind. Which is more than I can say for you. I was woken this morning by the sound of my hedge being cut down. And all for nothing."

She stood with her arm round Ping's shoulder, and he was astonished at her obstinate temper. He could feel her trembling. It was her garden, her bird sanctuary, her hedge and her visitor that she was defending. The men were ill at ease and would not willingly come again.

"I shall be glad", she said, "if you, Constable, will go and clear the crowds off my garden wall. It was never intended as a grandstand and is not safe."

"I quite understand your point of view, Madam, though we can't think you want the animal at large. People will gather wherever there is something to see—or nothing. We haven't a man to spare for controlling the footpath along the river, but I'll do what I can for you."

Major Blair put back the telephone. "The police dog will be here in half an hour from the aerodrome. Thank you, Mrs. Oldknow. I am sorry to have disturbed you."

The constable cleared the crowds off the wall, but they were back like flies as soon as his back was turned.

"At last we can have some breakfast. Are you hungry, Ping?"

"Yes. But I feel sick."

"You'll be better after breakfast. Open the door into the garden, please. At least no one can see us here. I'm sick of this public menagerie. We'll have an extra good breakfast to soothe us. But you do seem, my dear, to have been saying a little less than you know. It's better than saying more than you know, anyway. Shall I lay the table and you cook, or the other way round?"

"I'll lay, please." Ping was worried by the nearness outside the door of Hanno's hiding-place when he last saw him. Of course he could be anywhere in the garden now. He stepped out to listen. The hunt was apparently called off till the police dog should arrive. Men's voices could be heard arguing in the distance. Ping imagined the Keeper as the only one really worried. He felt a pang of conscience towards him. And yet, he thought, the Keeper would understand.

He laid the table with his eyes on the garden. It was a warm and exhilarating morning, as good as its promise. The sun streamed into the living room, the birds hopped in and out. Robin sat on the back of a chair and sang beneath his breath. His eldest fledgeling chirped on the threshold but dared not follow him in.

Mrs. Oldknow brought in steaming coffee and bacon that had scarcely stopped frizzling, crisp and appetizing. Ping sat in his usual place with the open door behind him.

"I don't believe you slept at all last night, Ping. The storm went on till about three o'clock this morning. How early did you get up? You were before me."

"About five, I should think. But I didn't go outside the garden."

147

"Were you all early birds last year, you and Ida and Oskar?"

"Oh yes. Very early. It was always the best time."

"Tell me some of the things you did."

Warmed by the coffee and bacon, Ping began to talk. It took his mind off the feeling that all was lost. It would also help to keep Mrs. Oldknow's eyes off the garden. She was extremely interested to know what adventures had happened at Green Knowe in her absence. She listened and enjoyed Ping's crisp imaginative telling. He had reached an important event, when he became aware that she was not attending. Her eyes were directed over the top of his shoulder, and the sunlight that had been shining on him through the doorway was suddenly cut off. As he looked up, she said quietly:

"Don't move, Ping. Take no notice. Just go on as before. *He's here*. In the doorway."

Her face was so lit up with excitement that the wrinkles seemed tensed away. She looked childlike, with that concentration of astonished curiosity that leaves no room for any other feeling.

Hanno stood resting his arm against the doorpost, his great head searching the room. He dwarfed the opening. He loomed like a natural force of the first order, causing the same thrill of recognition that a bather gives to an immense wave that has pulled up out of the ocean and suddenly towers hissing over him. It was impossible to see Hanno without taking in at the same time the dominance of the equatorial sun, the frier of the earth. The weight of silence in a thousand miles of forest, the ruthless interchange of life and death, are a millennium without time.

All this precipitated itself into the room, taking, on all fours, a more familiar form of wildness.

"Don't move, Ping."

The old lady neither moved nor spoke. She received the full impact of Hanno's eyes which combined the directness of a lion's stare with the interchange of a man's. He had sagaciously tested the atmosphere before entering a possible trap. Green Knowe smelled of stone, of flowers, of wood smoke, of coffee, but nothing of a zoo, and Ping was there eating.

Ping cast his eye over the table. He took a long loaf of plaited bread and held it out. It was taken like the torch in a relay race, and the startling visitor withdrew, pausing only to give Ping a word of command.

"I'm sorry," said Ping to his hostess. "I had to give him the biggest thing to keep him quiet for a bit. But I think he was looking for me. I'm afraid he will come back. Hadn't I better go to him?"

The old lady had lost her rosy colour and was growing frighteningly white, so that Ping checked himself and stayed with her.

"Now I think I understand everything," she said faintly. "Ping darling, the game is up. Think of all those people at the front. Something dreadful will happen. You must help the keeper to get him safely home. Go and find the Keeper. Tell *him*. Don't tell anyone else. There's no forest for Hanno, poor splendid thing. Only a tight little urban overbuilt England. Go now, Ping. It's the only thing you can do for him. I would go myself, but I can't trust my legs."

Ping ran out at the other side of the house as near sobbing as he had ever been in his life. Was it to be he who in the end gave Hanno up? It was an impossible thing to do. Even if he agreed it was the only possible end, his body would not have obeyed him, his tongue would refuse to speak. He ran, looking for nothing but a place to weep.

Now it happened that while this commotion was engaging the eastern side of Green Knowe, on the other side in the next hamlet there had been a small domestic mishap. A cow had calved in the field during the storm of the evening before, and having had the pleasure of her calf for so many hours, was unwilling to part with it when the farmer and his boy came to take it away. She ran head down at them again and again, keeping between them and the calf. More men were brought, but having won the first skirmish her blood was up. She attacked again, bellowing high screeches, but was shouted at, whacked, danced in front of and hit on the face, belaboured from all sides, outwitted and separated from her calf, till at last she charged about quite beside herself, not knowing what she was doing. She broke away from her tormentors and galloped along the river path with high, mad, female moos. Ping, sent on an errand he couldn't do, with his heart contracted to a dry clutch of pain was in the garden only vaguely aware of shouting crowds jumping over the garden wall and jostling to get through the gate. He thought of them only as Hanno's pursuers, thought Hanno must have shown himself on that side and that the crowds were surging to watch the capture or be in at the death. The cow swerved in at the gate and came at its lunatic unnatural gallop across the lawns straight for him. Just in time he came to himself and ran for dear life towards the nearest shelter, into the inner garden towards the bole of the big yew tree, too out of breath to pick his feet up properly. He tripped over the yew roots and sprawled headlong in the gravel. He gave himself up and waited to feel the horn in his ribs. But out of the branches came a whirling thunderbolt, flung with a spitting snarl between him and the cow. She stopped in her tracks, head down, swaying and uncertain. Hanno took her by the horns, his shoulder muscles twitched, and he had flipped her over on her back, her neck broken like a stick. He stood there roused and excited, ready for more, not wasting a second glance at the cow. What he did needed no confirmation.

Ping was still panting on the ground, blood flowing from his nose and arms when the farmer and his men all with sticks came round the dividing hedge in pursuit of the cow. When they saw who was standing waiting for them, they fled like starlings, but one had breath enough to shout—"The boy! There's a boy! Save the boy! Major! Here!" From all round voices shouted "The gorilla! He's got a boy. He's mauled a boy." Major Blair appeared with his gun, urged by the pointing arms of those who fled. A tide of people retreated at full speed from the garden.

And now Hanno saw again, face to face, his well remembered enemy, the man who had killed his father and taken himself and his sister captive. His heart swelled with a fury that was like a great joy. He stood to avenge these wrongs. He was his own drummer, beating his passionate chest, his own herald with that roar so horrifying that it can never be described, presenting himself for single combat against all comers and this one in particular who was due to be torn limb from limb. He gave fair warning, but before he had launched his onslaught the unfair bullet tore at his heart. He put his hands to his breast and pitched face downwards on the ground. In less than a split second all that was Hanno had ceased to exist.

The Keeper, who had got there as if by instinct, but too late, now helped the Major to turn him over. He looked with grim sorrow at the thirteen-year-old forest face from which all savagery had gone. For a gorilla never looks so tragically human as in the moment of death. Ping looked too, but not

Ping's Protector

for long. He went indoors to look for Mrs. Oldknow. She had been upstairs at the front of the house, trying to make out what was going on. She had seen the cow charge across the garden, had heard the shouts, the roar, the shot. And now she saw with overwhelming relief and affection Ping walking with a deliberate jauntiness towards her, his face set like a pale pebble under its smear of blood, his eyes hard like stars in a frost.

"He's dead," he said clearly and too composedly. "It's all right. That is how much he didn't want to go back, I saw him choose."

The old lady put her arm on his shoulder as if she, not he, needed support. The tide of people was now pouring back into the garden. They ran helter-skelter across lawns and beds. It was a wonder where they all came from. A gorilla had died there, something they dared not meet alive could be seen now dead, without danger. This event had turned them all into primitive tribesmen running to exult. Private property had ceased to exist. But Mrs. Oldknow no longer minded. Ping was telling her what had happened. Out of the window they could see cars and brakes driving up, groups of men in conference, messengers sent off and more and more running towards the inner garden.

Under the window the Keeper with Major Blair and the Police Inspector crossed the front of the house and rang the bell.

"We had better both go," she said. "You can tell them everything now."

"We have come to inquire about the boy," said the white-faced Keeper. "Is he hurt?"

"Not at all, I'm glad to say." Mrs. Oldknow pushed Ping forward. "It's only scratches and a nose bleed. It might have been much worse."

"I am glad. This has been a nightmare to me for the last three days. I'm the one responsible for everything Hanno does—did. Didn't I see you at the Zoo not so long ago, young man, in front of his cage?"

"Yes."

"And you've been sharing the Thicket with him ever since he escaped, all unknowing?"

"No, I knew."

"Come in please," said Mrs. Oldknow. "Ping is ready to tell you all about it."

The Inspector and Major Blair excused themselves. "We are happy to know there has been no accident." (Ping and the Keeper found they were looking at each other and agreed by sympathy that no statement could have been more untrue). "If you will excuse us, Mrs. Oldknow, we will try to clear your garden of crowds and get the carcasses away. It has been very alarming for you, and but for Major Blair might have been much worse. He certainly saved the boy's life."

Mrs. Oldknow could not bring herself to say the expected complimentary thanks. She merely bowed them away.

"That was not true," she said when she had made the Keeper sit down. "It was Hanno who saved Ping from being gored. It was to protect Ping that he would have charged. There was no need to have shot him. It was all a mistake." In this she was wrong. Hanno had his own account to settle.

The Keeper beat his fists one upon the other. Some mistakes are hard to bear. Ping stood near him in fellow feeling.

"He was very happy in the Thicket, quite private and at home. I took him food because I was afraid he might eat yew branches. I remembered everything you had said and tried to do it. And then he seemed to want gorilla company, so I had to be a little gorilla and do what I was told. Then it began to be harder to look after him. So I tried pretending to be attacked by a snake or something to see if it would make him run to me, and it did. But when he found it was for nothing he cuffed me. Look—see? But the cow was real."

"If you had told at the beginning, this would never have happened."

"If I had told, he would never have had his three real days, not in all his life."

The Keeper sighed in mixed exasperation and understanding. "You've given me the three worst days I've ever had in mine. I was fond of him, you know."

"I watched him when you were calling him. He hated not going to you."

"Do you know how he got out of the Thicket?"

"I showed him a bridge. A tree blew down in the night. He followed me across it."

"May I ask, Madam, if you knew anything about this?"

"Nothing at all till Hanno joined me at breakfast. I looked up, and there he was in the doorway. I should have guessed before, I knew Ping had a secret. I knew he took food. The facts were all before me. He almost told me. But some things are impossible to believe. As soon as I knew I sent Ping to tell you, but the cow intervened. Let Ping get us some coffee—we are all badly shocked. Then you can get all the details from him. Wash your face, Ping, dear. You look awful."

Ping hurried to serve, while the old lady told all she knew. Then he was cross-examined, standing before the Keeper and telling the exact truth from beginning to end.

"I envy you, young man," said the Keeper magnanimously when he had finished. "And I admire your nerve. And maybe we are the only two who really mind what has happened. You could get into trouble with the police for lying to them,

"I envy you, young man".

but I'll do my best to prevent it. I don't think you'll hear any more about it. Come and see me some time at the Zoo. Maybe", he said sadly, "I'll be given another youngster to bring up, or better still two, that you could play with. They are not so unhappy as you think. But of course there should be two."

When the Keeper had gone, Mrs. Oldknow drew Ping to her.

"I've been thinking," she said, "I wonder how much *you* mind 'going back' as you said about Hanno. Would you like to live here with Tolly and me? Because I really feel I can't do without you. Would you?"

Ping gasped, blushed, and nodded.

"And until Tolly comes, I think we must try to get Ida. If I write to her parents I am sure they will let her come."

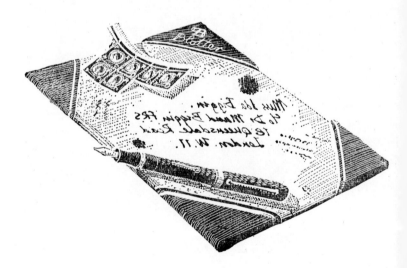